Blood Empire

Blood Empire

A Season of Seduction & Revenge

SYDNEY KNOX

Followed by:
Blood Empire
Book Two:
A Time of Fear & Flight

Dedication

I thank God for blessing the works of my hand. May they be acceptable in His sight. For the people who matter in my life; my children Adrian, Christian and Corrie, my mother Iola Bigger whose support nourished me and my sister Eboney Foster, who is my conscience and when necessary my co-conspirator, I love you all dearly. You are my "why."

Table of Contents

Maps

ROMAN BRITANNIA

Map Acknowledgements

Britannia/Rome - Historical Atlas of William Shepherd, 1929 edition
Mediolanum courtesy of Lorenzo Fratti

MEDIOLANUM (Milan)

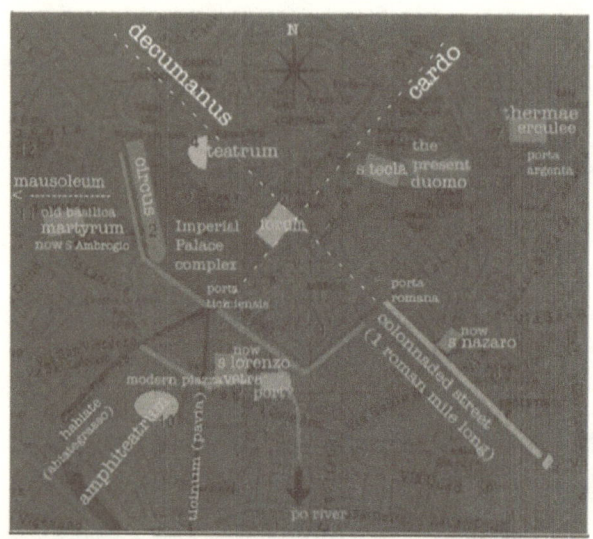

CENTER OF IMPERIAL ROME

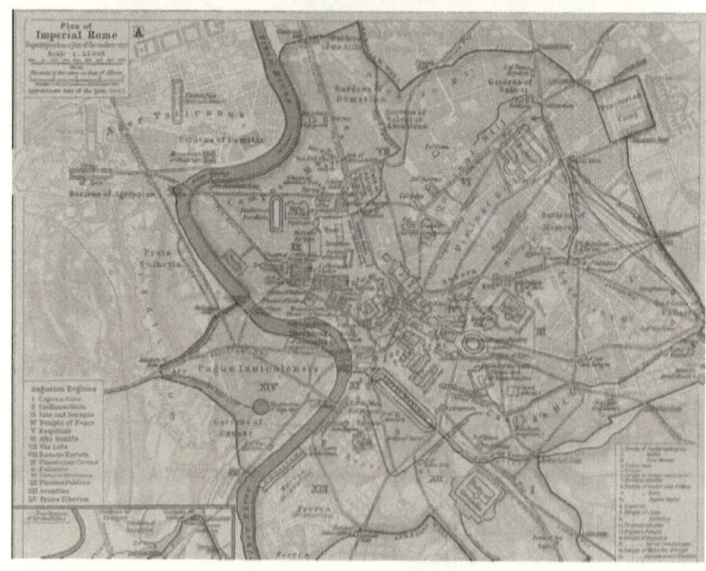

Chapter One:

The Emperor's Last Breath

July 25, 306 — Eboracum, Roman province of Britannia

"The emperor will be dead in an hour."

The surgeon's voice trembled as he made the fateful announcement.

The bedchamber went silent at the news. Constantius Chlorus had been the Western Augustus of Rome for less than two war seasons. A man of middle years, he lay on his sickbed looking as though life had fled him already. With so much of the world an unplucked fruit, he was not prepared to die. Worse, his death was an untimely one, which is never a simple matter in the high places of the world. When great men die, whether in a battle or a brothel, the people question it because it's unnatural for their immortals to perish.

And so it was for Constantius, who had the good sense (or bad luck depending on whom you asked) not to die in either a brothel or on a battlefield, but flat on his back. His impending death sparked a firestorm of dread that spread from his sick room to the legions outside its walls. No one could have imagined this tragedy and no one knew what to do.

Inside the crowded room of doctors and ranking officers, fear was more alive than the emperor. The room was heavy with frankincense to cover both the stench of death and the bitter aroma the doctor's potions left behind. Death was coming fast and sure for the battle-hardened commander. The first hint of trouble arrived with a chill a fortnight ago; yet there had been plenty of life in him until today. This morning he had awoke fevered, each breath sounding like his last.

His doctors stood in a corner, short on time and out of ideas. They wrung their hands, shifted in their tunics, and tried to appear busy saving a life already lost.

"What curse is this?" Constantius sputtered in his delirium.

Fragments of memory put him in the castra in North Britannia, with high walls and 5000 soldiers between him and the marauding tribesmen in rebellion against Rome. Normally the intervallum was still and quiet under the noonday sun, but today was different. Today, the field was abuzz with quiet muttering and whispers among the men.

"They say it's a passing fever, he'll recover in a few days…it's a ruse to lure the Picts to attack, he can't die…the general is just testing us…" But they believed little of their own optimistic babble. Unspoken was the single question on everyone's mind, "who will lead us now?"

Constantius shifted at the sounds of his men outside. His eyelids were heavy. Something pulled at him, sweeter than sleep. He dared not indulge it. He had seen too much of death not to recognize its breath on his neck. Yet, he had one stratagem to play before he surrendered to his final enemy.

A sliver of clarity broke through his fever. With great effort, Constantius raised up on his lectus[1]. In a faded remnant of his once commanding growl, he asked, "Where is Constantine?"

A voice rang out beside him. "Here, Caesar...Father."

Saving his strength, Constantius barely turned. "Come closer. Let us speak together for the last time." As their eyes met, the face his mother swore was so like his own in his youth struck Constantius as one he would miss. Father and son were both tall powerfully built men, with a heavy brow and protruding eyes, but where Constantius was hazel-eyed and fair-skinned, Constantine had his mother Helena's deep brown eyes and dark curly hair. Constantius never married Helena, but she was the love of his life, the woman whose child he readily proclaimed a son.

It had been 25 years before that morning, when Constantius met Helena in a tiny village in Bithynia. She was a tavern owner's daughter with no future prospects other than dying where she was born, until she met Constantius. The garrisoned legion where he was an ambitious and rising tribune was passing through on maneuvers. She served him rabbit stew and captured him on the spot with her exotic features and easy manner.

"You there, girl. Come sit with me, keep me company while I try your watery stew." Constantius

---

[1] Roman bed, usually entered by steps.

remembered the smell of the savory rabbit under his nose and Helena's brown eyes and freckled nose before him as she turned him down cold.

"I don't suffer rude men or soldiers... and you are both."

"But I'm more entertaining...come. I'll make you a gift if you will make me one, sit with me."

Constantius had laughed then and when after a moment she broke and giggled in spite of herself, he knew then it would not be the last time he made her happy.

He loved her that day and every day since and he loved their son. On the day Constantine was born, Constantius fell to his knees at Helena's bedside.

"Your gift is well received. I will treasure him as I treasure you," he told her, and he had never broken that promise.

In Constantius' fevered mind, he saw himself stroking her hair all those years ago. He could still smell the sweat of her labor over the trace of sweet myrrh that failed to mask it. It was glorious to him. His eyes opened at the thought. Unbidden, the dying man smiled.

Constantine knelt at his father's bedside and leaned in close. Constantius lifted a skeletal hand to touch his face.

The emperor began slowly, his voice no more than a murmur. "My son, I die with only one regret, that I did not better prepare you for the burden you must carry now. Rome's enemies gather as always, but I can do no more. Don't repeat my mistakes with your son. Make him know his purpose. You will succeed where I failed. I swear to you now; this was always my intention. Give me your hand."

Constantius' voice became stronger. With waxy fingers slick with sweat, he pulled off his signet ring. Placing it in Constantine's outstretched palm, he told him, "Finish what I have started." Then with a wavering hand, Constantius slid the ring onto Constantine's finger. When the emperor's hand dropped away, the ring remained, gleaming in the light. The imperial signet and all that came with it now belonged to Constantine.

Constantius shifted painfully and closed his eyes. He ached all over and passing Constantine his birthright had nearly drained him.

When he opened his eyes again, a new name formed on his lips. "Bring Julius."

On the other side of the room, Constantius' closest advisor, the general Julius Asclepiodotus, was haranguing the doctors. They cowered before him. Sunlight streaming through the narrow window above them revealed the general's handsome features twisted into a terrible mask of panic and rage. An asp to its prey, Julius snatched up an unlucky doctor by his tunic. The doctor yelped while the others cowered or fled. Julius reached for the sheathed dagger hanging at his waist. A metallic scrape sliced through the air while the tiny man tried to find air under Julius' clenched hand. The stench of murder in a death room filled the rancid air and a small puddle of urine formed at the doctor's feet.

Julius slowly raised his hand to strike but Constantine called the general to his senses.

"Julius! Leave the doctors alone. They can do no more. Your emperor is asking for you. Come." He ordered with new authority that raised Julius' head from his task.

Julius was the *Praefectus Praetorio²*, Constantius' his right hand of power and when necessary, his fist. He had been at his side for more years than either of them cared to remember.

"Useless fool! You should be dying instead my friend!" he hissed at the doctor and dropped the man to the floor in a quivering heap. Julius scowled at the man in disgust, stepping across the puddled urine on his way to his emperor's bedside.

"Sire...I am at your command!" he said, his voice thick with emotion.

Constantius tried to speak but was suddenly wracked with a fit of coughing. Quickly Julius demanded water for his best friend and commander. He held the cup while Constantius sat up to swallow a mouthful.

"Help my son take what is his," he whispered, falling back to his pillow.

Julius' face crumpled at the words he did not want to hear. He pleaded with Constantius. "Brother! You have fought in too many battles to meet your end this way. Rise from this bed and let us see this campaign to its end!" His resolve broke and he dropped to one knee at the bedside. Before a sob could escape to humiliate him, Constantius shook his head, stopping him without a word and as always, Julius obeyed without a question.

"On my life, I swear I will not fail you!" Julius leaned forward to kiss the imperial ring, but it was gone from his emperor's hand. He turned to Constantine, who raised his own hand to confirm the

---

²Praetorian Perfect, the commander of the most elite soldiers of the empire, the emperor's personal guards.

deed. Standing together at his bedside, they watched as Constantius' chest rose once more then slowly fell.

"Helena…my Helena," he murmured. The air drained from his body along with his life and the legendary Augustus Constantius went still.

His son's life took on a completely new meaning at his death. In passing his signet ring to Constantine, the emperor sealed the succession for his eldest son over his children by his lawful wife, Theodora. With this single act, Constantine's illegitimate birth no longer mattered. His father chose him. He now had the undeniable right to seek the title Augustus, Emperor of the West.

The lute player sent to comfort the emperor stopped strumming. Constantine passed his hand over his father's face and closed the eyes that were once feared by kings and slaves alike. Constantius' face was soft to the touch and still warm. He seemed merely asleep. The illusion only lasted a moment, before it was broken by the appearance of Aristos, the emperor's devoted body slave. The grief-stricken old man crumbled against the doorframe, his face a mask of grief.

"Dominus," he moaned. He fell to his knees and would have crawled sobbing to his master's side had Constantine not pulled him roughly to his feet.

"None of that, Aristos. My father would not have you so…and neither will I."

Aristos nodded. He wiped away his tears, but fresh ones appeared in their place. Constantine looked away. Tears were a luxury they could not afford to indulge. His father had many enemies; no one close to him was safe.

Constantine issued brisk orders. "Aristos, I want my father's funeral organized immediately. Send word to my son Crispus, and my half-brothers and sisters in Treverorum. Send for them at once, their mother too, if she will come. Keep the news quiet otherwise. No one else outside this castra must know the emperor is dead yet. Julius, come with me." Constantine left the room with his eyes dry and his head high, his father's son in every way.

Julius touched his friend's hand one last time then followed Constantine from the room.

Outside in the shadows of the hallway, with only the cold stone to overhear them, he spoke in stark terms. "I will announce my claim as Augustus of the West immediately. And the legions will need a firm hand until I am ready to march south. Tell me, can you truly lead this army now?"

Julius reared up with wounded pride. "I have served your father since he and I were only boys playing at war! Of course I can lead this army, and lead it to victory. But," he emphasized with a raised hand, "I expect Emperors Maximian and Galerius will move to seize your men and lands as soon as they hear of this. Your father's death leaves a gaping hole in the tetrarchy. The Senate will unite against you if we're not careful, and you will not be recognized as his heir until—"

"Then it is crucial we move quickly," Constantine said, cutting him off. "True, there will be some who reject my claim – Maximian and Galerius first among them. But they can't unite against us if we set them at each other's throats. While they squabble over the spoils of Britannia, I'll gather support among the Italian legions. Then we shall see who they follow into battle in the homeland."

Julius nodded, then added, "–and from Italia to the rest of the empire. Your father would approve."

Constantine led Julius further down the stone corridor, stopping before the deep red curtains that marked the doorway of the most sacred room in the castra, Constantius' war chamber.

The war room had seen historic meetings before now. Here the war council plotted feats of bravery and celebrated Constantius' victories in Britannia. A Praetorian snapped sharply to attention as they approached, his sword clanging against the wall behind him. The man's face betrayed recent anguish; Constantius' men loved him. Constantine and the Praetorian shared an instant of mutual grief in their salutes to each other, executed to perfection; a proud tribute to the father they both lost with Constantius' untimely death.

The small space was immaculately clean and utilitarian. The simple Carrara marble desk sat atop an aged, but expensive-looking rug depicting King Philip in the Battle of Chaeronea in faded shades of blue. Backless chairs were scattered throughout. Two armaria stood open in the corners, each holding neatly arranged codices of Greek texts, organized by subject. Constantius was an eager student of philosophy and literature, passions he passed on to Constantine. 'An educated man will always triumph over those who know nothing,' he told him.

Constantine and Julius stood side by side just inside the doorway. The enormity of what had happened made the chamber feel hollow, never again to be filled with the booming laughter and quiet commands of Constantius Chlorus. The essence of his mystique lingered though, left behind as sure as the hint of the cypress and lemongrass oils he favored. Constantine found a place to rest his eyes lest they betray and shame him as Julius' had nearly done in the emperor's death chamber.

In a room for planning a war, seats of power are plentiful, though some were more special than others were. Of every chair in the room, there was only one that truly mattered, Constantius' handcrafted sella curulis[3], unlike any other in the world. The seat of power in Britannia was made of iron forged in Rome. It was tall and sturdy with a black leather latticework back and padded arms. Constantius demanded the metal frame be shined daily, and so it gleamed in black glory as Constantine and Julius entered the room.

On the wall above it was the world Constantine had just inherited. Spanning corner to corner, an aged map covered the entirety of the Roman Empire; from the wilderness of Britannia to the fertile North African coastline and beyond, to the Eastern provinces of Pontus, Macedonia and Judea.

Without a word, Constantine took his father's chair. Within the walls of the castra at least, he was now the Augustus of the West with all the wealth and power of the position in his hands. He hesitated a heartbeat of time, and then leaned back into the chair. Shifting his weight against the supple embrace of the leathers, he settled into the seat of power.

---

[3] Curule chair, seat of power used by Roman leaders holding Imperium, the command of an army

The sella curulis rose in majesty behind Constantine, and he ran his fingers along its buckskinned arms. He breathed deeply, letting the essence of his father's authority drift down upon him. This was the moment for which he was born, to secure his family's legacy. With nothing left to lose and the entire world to gain, he was finally ready.

Julius took his place in front of his new emperor, to bear witness as the mantle of power came to rest on Constantine's shoulders rather than his own. Julius always knew of Constantius' plans and he raised no quarrel with his choice. No hour in life would ever be as beautiful or bittersweet for either of them.

Julius spoke first, his voice low and urgent, his words tumbling from his lips, seeking a target. "So you will be Augustus of the West, good. Now what? Because there will be trouble as soon as you announce it. Where will it come from first? Your father's enemies in the senate are yours now too. Those loyal to Maximian and his son are few, a boon for our cause but it's the moderates you must reckon with. For the fools who openly oppose you, I say run the streets red with the blood of a few of them and the rest will fall in line."

Constantine shook his head. "It's not the senate we have to worry about – this conflict won't be decided in the Curia – or even the threat of Maximian and his brat Maxentius. No, I'll have to contend with Galerius as the first order of business. He is Augustus of the East and the senior emperor. If I intend any move he must be agreeable to it or made to keep quiet his discontent at least."

"No better way than to get rid of his friends." Julius suggested hopefully.

Constantine dismissed the notion with a wave of his hand; the imperial signet ring flashed in the light. "I won't be a butcher unless I have to. That would sully the whole affair. There is another way. If I can maneuver Galerius into recognizing my claim, I'm well-situated to resist any challenges if there is a hackle raised over it in the senate. If the Augustus recognizes me, everyone else will be forced to fall in line."

"What are your thoughts then?" Julius asked curious to know how Constantine intended to win over a man known for bloodthirstiness without spilling any.

"When you send Galerius the news of my father's death, send it along with my request to stand as Augustus of the West in his place. Tell him my father's legions demand it, and I must accept, with his consent of course." Constantine finished, with a satisfied smirk playing at the corners of his mouth.

Julius expressed his doubts. "Galerius is a prideful man. He will say this hubris. By the gods, I would call it hubris too! I've never seen him submit without a fight. I'm not sure if a threat hidden behind humility is the best way to persuade him."

"I don't need to persuade him, Julius. I just need him to stay silent. Whether he is insulted or not, Galerius is no fool. I was his tribune and I'm familiar with his tactics. With an army at my back, he will have to reckon with me or risk an embarrassing defeat. It would be worse than when I escaped him to come to my father in the first place."

Julius chuckled. The soldiers of the castra still talked about it around the fires, the story was legend. Constantine escaped from his hostage post under Galerius by getting him drunk and hamstringing every horse in the stables before he fled the city. By the time Galerius woke and summoned his Praetorians, it was too late. Constantine was beyond his reach and heading to his father, wiser and less trusting of allies after that.

"You know the man. I will give you that, but then what of Maximian? The man is slipperier than a moray eel."

"Maximian is officially in retirement. Galerius is the only living Augustus. Maximian can do nothing without his help. This way I slay two lions with a single arrow. Galerius may balk at a demand to be proclaimed Augustus of the West true enough, but he will consent to allow me to take power as a Caesar in the wake of it, and that will do for now."

"Caesar? You will play second when first is within your grasp? Rome was not founded on timid acts. You would not be the first to impose your will with a sword at someone's throat!"

Constantine spoke with care. "Battle lust has its place my friend, but this is politics. It requires a different sort of warfare." Trying to explain politics to Julius was a difficult task, but Constantine tried as usual to explain details to a man by nature uncomfortable with them. "What I gain is legitimacy. If Galerius proclaims me, I immediately become eligible of both offices because what is Caesar but a stepping-stone to Augustus? The way need not be greased with blood when guile will work better."

"Well, it seems you have thought of everything," Julius said with pride. "Your father would agree with you. He was always one to use strategy over brawn. I prefer to knock heads together and figure out the politics later but that is me." Julius shrugged in mock resignation.

"–And I am of different sort, Julius. I have a plan. I intend to execute it."

Constantine got up from the chair. He paced the narrow room, deep in thought. No longer a fresh-faced tribune; now he was a general and an emperor of Rome at a time when that meant being one of four men.

It was Diocletian, a man as cruel as he was brilliant, who split rule of the empire. He took the title Augustus of the East and selected his friend Marcus Maximian to rule beside him as Augustus of the West. They chose two as Caesars to rule under them, groomed to take their place one day. It was a plan elegant in its simplicity, and like most misguided ideas, it began well.

The tetrarchy was in its second decade when Diocletian retired alongside Maximian and Constantius became the Augustus of the West, with the Dacian hero, Galerius holding the East. Employing a time honored tradition; Maximian adopted Constantius as a son and gave him his daughter Theodora as a wife.

With Diocletian and Maximian retired, the design was for the sons of Constantius and Maximian to rule after them, but Galerius with characteristic flair sabotaged that plan. Two of his devoted lackeys were chosen instead, with vague and insulting promises that Constantine and Maxentius would rule later tossed in to ease the indignity.

That was how the tetrarchy should have played out, but tragic circumstances now yielded a more promising path to greatness. Destiny provided an opportunity for Constantius' death to correct the slight on Constantine with his father's marriage to Theodora and his forced abandonment of Helena.

With his father's legions at his back and clever strategy, Constantine could avenge himself and solidify the House of Constantius into the supreme authority in Rome. A dynastic crisis was approaching, and the fate of the known world hinged on the outcome. Constantine was eager to show he was strong enough to carry the burden.

But first, he had to give his father to the flames.

Chapter Two:

The Fires of Fortune

The former Augustus Maximian lived in seclusion in Paestum, a charming little town at the edge of the Tyrrhenian Sea, only 200 miles from Rome. His was a forced retirement and it bored him to no end. His sixty summers had diminished none of his passions. His slaves were his only amusement, and they too became tiresome once his lust was sated. That was not the case this day. Maximian lay in the midst of his lemon trees in a hammock, naked except for his subligaria[4] and cuddling a serving girl when a message arrived that changed his fortunes.

He was just settling in for a nap across her pale breasts, that were just beginning to melon in the bloom of womanhood. A courier rushed across the garden to deliver an urgent message. It was from his daughter Theodora. Her short letter said soldiers from Eboracum had brought her news. Her worst fears were confirmed and Maximian was presented with an opportunity to change his legacy if he dared to seize it;

---

[4] Undergarment worn by both men and women, a loincloth

Dearest father,

Constantius is dead of a fever in the North and I am in Treverorum alone. Constantine has sent for me but who can say if your grandchildren and I are safe? You must demand he return me to your protection after the funeral. Please help me father.

I remain your devoted daughter.
Theodora

He clicked his tongue as he read. "Well now, that *is* interesting!" He cared very little for Theodora and her children to return to his household. 'Though, I suppose I must allow it,' he thought. His eldest daughter had always been a plague on him, but Constantius' death – now that was surprising and prodigious news indeed.

Maximian gave the servant girl, barely in her teens, a sweetmeat and sent her back into the house with a slap on her rear. He fell back into his hammock with his eyes closed, savoring the promise of another chance at his heart's desire, hidden within the crumpled letter in his hands. Constantius' death provided a reason to escape from the tedium of his retirement; an act of divine providence if he ever saw one.

Following the girl inside the villa, he roamed the sprawling complex for hours, lost in his schemes amidst the masterpieces of his art collection. A great lover of beauty, Maximian surrounded himself with examples of it in both handsome slaves and fine works of art. As he walked the colorful mosaics on the floors in endless circles; he passed exquisite busts, statues and expertly woven tapestries depicting his storied victories. He was so taken by his schemes, he hardly noticed them. When at length the dawn arrived, it found him in the quiet splendor of his peristyle garden amid the sculptures of Diana and her nymphs at play. Finding a resting place on one of the surrounding couches, he lay down to sleep at last.

The lush greenery of dwarf Cypress trees and the various blooming roses, orchids and ferns of the garden enveloped him in peaceful solitude. He needed it after such a long night, as his mind birthed and discarded a hundred different plots and scenarios before settling on one. It was risky, this plan, but it would place a purple robe on his shoulders again and secure the same for Maxentius, even if the wretch did not deserve it.

Standing in his way was Galerius, the 'Dacian fox' as Maximian called him. If Maximian could maneuver Constantine into opposing Galerius, Constantine would take care of his problem for him. To ensure it, Maximian decided to bless the fraudulent enterprise with a marriage. His daughter Fausta was an obvious choice as wife to Constantine, had been for years. It was time to make the idle talk a reality. Once Fausta captured his heart, an easy thing for her, Maximian would own him as well.

His strategy set, he begged the god Somnus to give him rest. Yet the guardian of sleep resisted his pleas. He lay watching as the aging arms of ebony night loosed the morning from its clutches. The rays of light on the stone fountain gurgling next to him morphed from pink to orange and then at last dazzling sunlight as day broke across the sky. He dozed fitfully only to awake at the slap of sandals on tile as Avelina, his hammock girl and favorite this month appeared in the garden with food and drink.

"Jentaculum is served, Dominus," she said with lowered eyes. She had changed into a fresh tunic and was even lovelier now than she had been in the evening mist. He looked at her with sudden lust; but just as quickly, the feeling passed him by on its way to somewhere more fun. 'If I weren't so tired...' he mused.

Her youth was intoxicating. She had soft, straw-colored curls and pale skin typical of Germanic beauties like her. But right now, the tray of food she carried in her slender arms was an immediate need for him. She brought him a large bowl of fruit salad with grapes, figs and cantaloupe, an assortment of fresh oysters and fish, bread and honey. To quench his thirst, a boy followed behind her with amphorae of fruit juices, wine, and water.

"Leave it there, girl." Maximian pointed to a small table a few feet from where he lay. "I think I'll rest here a while longer before I eat. Is my son here yet? I thought he was due to arrive from Rome today."

"Yes, Dominus. He arrived only a few moments ago. I believe he has gone to the baths. Shall I ask him to come to you when he is finished?" Avelina sat down her tray and poured Maximian a cup of wine that she mixed heavily with water.

"No, I'll speak to him later this afternoon. It's much too tiresome to bother with him now. Leave me and see that I'm not disturbed." Maximian dipped a crust of the bread into a small pot of honey and washed it down with the wine she handed him.

"Dominus," Avelina nodded, glad to leave him. She had seen the look in his eyes. Though, the old Dominus was better than his son. Every servant in the villa dreaded the arrival of Maxentius. The last time he visited his father, he had beaten bloody a young girl who dared to cry when he dragged her to his bed. Maximian was a regrettable nuisance to the female slaves and a few of the more good-looking boys, but he was never excessively cruel. To their sorrow, Maxentius was a danger to endure.

Late in the afternoon Maximian appeared in one of the dining rooms, reinvigorated and freshly bathed. He reclined on a couch with a look of annoyance on his face. Maxentius was nowhere in sight, though raucous laughter and feminine squeals of delight could be heard all through the villa. Maximian questioned a passing clerk who was scurrying to the library, his arms full of scrolls.

The man cleared his throat. "Dominus, it's your son. He is occupied with Senator Lucius Rufinius' daughter, Mistress Caesonia."

"Caesonia again? That she-wolf! I had no notion she was in the city. She is a beauty I suppose, but that doesn't matter. Inform my son that I want him here now even if he is in *flagrante delicto*.[5]" He stopped to raise a hand in caution. "Say nothing to Caesonia, her father is an important client."

"As you command, Dominus." The man left the room jostling his scrolls in his arms, and returned

---

[5] From the Latin, meaning literally, 'in blazing offence', caught in the act

a short while later with a slightly tousled and very annoyed Maxentius in tow.

"I hope this is urgent. You cut short my fun. Caesonia has a Macedonian tongue trick she wants to show me – you're ruining a promising afternoon for me." He glared at his father before tossing himself down on the opposite couch with a huff.

"That is of no consequence." Maximian dismissed his objections with a wave of his hand. "I'll invite her to visit again; the slut will be happy to comply. She can show you her tongue tricks then, but if you ever want to be emperor, cease your whining and listen to me. Your chance has finally arrived, courtesy of Constantius."

"Eh? What's he done now? I thought that old badger was still in Britannia."

"He is in Britannia, and he will never leave it. He's dead, your sister writes that a fever took him not a fortnight ago. A fever! After so many years of war and bloodshed. Ironic." Maximian chuckled to himself. Stretching forward for his wine, he drained the cup.

A serving boy arrived with a heavy platter of oysters, freshly steamed in their shells. They filled the air with a strong, salty aroma. Maximian immediately reached for the garum jar and poured the thick fish sauce over of the oysters before slurping down a few. He finished with a loud gulp.

"Delicious," he murmured. In the excitement of finally telling his son his plans, he found his appetite had returned with gusto.

Maxentius shrugged. "Constantius dead? That's sudden news sure, but what is it to me? You aren't going to suggest I try to take his place, are you?

Not yet at least." Maxentius turned away more interested in the platter in front of him, he waited in silence for his father to grab another oyster before reaching for one of the largest for himself. He inhaled for a moment, enjoying the tangy scent then slid it warm and wet down his throat. He reached immediately for another one and did the same.

Maximian frowned at his son, watching him inhaling oysters while he tried to hand him an empire. "And why not, pray tell? It's high time you started living up to your responsibilities instead of meddling on the edge of politics."

Maxentius swallowed his oyster so that he could speak. "I do not meddle on the edge! I'll have you know, father I've been busy forming alliances in the senate. I'll make my move when the time is right." Maxentius paused to consider something else. "And besides, what of the other tetrarchs in this great plan of yours? What you suggest is folly born of your pining for past glories. It is impossible!"

"Difficult perhaps, but not impossible for a man of purpose. It requires no more than a cunning mind and an iron will. Yours has grown soft of late, taken with wine and women. You have plenty of guile left in you, my boy. Use it for more than seducing senators' daughters for once!" Maximian was nearly shouting, he stopped to calm himself before he continued.

"Constantine will need help if he plans to take Constantius' place as Augustus. We must form an alliance with him, and offer him your sister as a sweetener. When he is comfortable and happy, we strike and usurp him."

"There is no reason for Constantine to trust such an arrangement. The time is not ripe for this, Father."

Maximian turned sharp again. "There will never be a more opportune time, Maxentius! Fortuna seldom rewards the lazy or fearful."

He went on laying out his plan, oblivious to Maxentius' complaints, which slowed the more he ate, drank and listened to his father.

The two whispered long into the evening; dark conspiracies blooming between them like so many poisonous little poppies. Over an endlessly full table, Maximian sold his son the vision of a glorious dynasty that would last a thousand years. And Maxentius swallowed it whole just he had the oysters.

At the Roman castra in Eboracum …

In the gray dreariness of an overcast day, the full legion of 5000 men gathered at noon in the yard of the praetorium to send off one of their own. Flavius Valerius Constantius Herculius Augustus, called in casual terms Constantius Chlorus, was a father to them all. The piles of tribute stacked before his family bore witness to his soldiers' devotion.

Emperor Constantius lay on a white oak pyre that rose ten feet into the air. His body was draped in purple silk and his eyes were stitched closed. For tradition, he held a coin for the boatman Charon in his mouth. His sword and personal armor lay atop his chest to be consumed in the flames with him. The death masks of his noble ancestors were arrayed before the funeral pyre, the renowned Emperor Claudius Gothicus among them.

Behind the pyre was a seating area for family, friends and the various dignitaries who made the arduous trip from Rome and points beyond. Constantine stood beside Crispus, his only child and commander of his Germanic legions. He had arrived from the Rhine frontier to bid farewell to the grandfather he adored. Riding hard and fast, Crispus made certain he was at Constantine's side when they burned his father's body.

And while Crispus was front and center, Constantius' wife Theodora was shunted off to one side along with her children. It was a humiliating placement at her husband's funeral, though her pride did not allow her to acknowledge the slight. She was in formal disarray, her long dark curls left unruly as custom dictated, and dressed in a simple black sleeveless stola. Despite the heat, a black shawl was draped over her exposed shoulders. The hand of her eldest son held her steady. Her son should have been Constantius' lawful heir; instead, his youth and inexperience meant Theodora had to accept Constantine's authority and the indignity that came with it.

Flavius Dalmatius, a bright, strapping boy of fifteen summers, was the very image of Constantius, more so than his four siblings, who shared the exotic coloring of their mother. Constantius' family was young and beautiful, more so in their grief. They all woke the shocked expression of one still expecting to wake up from a dream.

Even the heavens grieved the loss of Constantius. The gray skies burst open and a drizzling rain fell over the assembly. The time had come to send the great man on his way.

Constantine stepped forward to give his eulogy. He bowed his head as if seeking divine inspiration. A commotion rose among the ranks of men as some of them howled in desolation. Constantine quieted them with a raised hand. When all was silent, he began:

My brothers,

Of my father – what can I say about this hero of the people? Through his honest character, he was committed to the perseverance of our Roman supremacy, of our state pride. He lived each day as if it were his last and made all of them count towards the shared cause of every good Roman.

A more noble man has not lived since the days of our great republic and I salute him with my whole heart. So strenuously did he perform the duties of his office that there are none to complain of receiving injustice at his hands...

I pray the gods of Rome and the god of my mother, grant him rest and protection. And in his place, I pray you soldiers assembled here will give me your loyalty. I know he would have it so and here is the proof.

He raised his hand to show the imperial signet. The men gave a cheer. Theodora gasped and Flavius Dalmatius eyes went wide, then flooded with shamed tears at the betrayal. He did nothing to stop them from running down his face as Julius handed

Constantine a burning torch. He laid it gently against the wooden frame and the funeral pyre blazed into flames so brilliant they challenged the morning. Even the drizzling rain could not dampen them. Those gathered shielded their eyes. The professional mourners stepped forward to begin grief-filled dirges in both Latin and Greek. They were beautiful, and heartbreaking to hear. As Constantius' body burned, the singers wailed, and in the audience, more than the children cried. Every life there was touched in some way by Constantius Chlorus and was better for it.

Moved by sentiment, Constantine went to his stepmother Theodora. He kissed her on each cheek.

"Dear lady, you have lost much this day. You need have no fear of me. Your children are my blood and I promise to protect them and you. In return, all I ask is that you honor Constantius' memory. Pledge your loyalty to me." He stretched out his hand. His father's signet gleamed in the light.

Theodora could only accept his hand with as much grace as her stomach would allow. Shaking a little as she did it, she leaned forward to brush her lips against the ring.

In a hoarse whisper, "I pledge to you Constantine..." She would have choked on the words but for her breeding, "–My emperor, that my children and I will follow you faithfully. Or may death take us all." Beside her, her boys squirmed in embarrassment for her. They looked away from the spectacle, but Theodora's face betrayed no emotion. Satisfied with her capitulation, Constantine moved back in his place to whisper in Julius' ear.

"My father's season is over. This one belongs to me and the real work begins now."

Chapter Three:

Bellum Conventus ad Mediolanum
(War Council in Milan)

Three years later...

Augustus Maximian's palace in Mediolanum was unique in the extravagant way all such places are unique, and yet all the same. It was as smug an expression of self-indulgence as one might expect from a man whose aim was to mark the whole city with his image. His palace was his crowning achievement in a twenty-year building campaign.

When Maximian arrived in the year 285, he found Mediolanum a city of traders with an admitted semblance of industry, but an unattractive backwater nonetheless. He promptly went to work to correct the problem. Now, a glorious cosmopolis had sprung up, marked by an amphitheater, basilicas and baths renowned as some of the most structurally beautiful outside of Rome.

Perched in the middle lands between the Alps and the River Padus, Mediolanum was an ideal project for an ambitious ruler. But though Maximian left an indelible mark on the landscape; the hearts of the people were a different matter. What began as a love affair soured as the radiance of his public works were eclipsed by the crushing taxes he imposed to finish them. When Constantine's army arrived in 309, it was no wonder the citizenry threw open the gates to welcome him. Constantine's reputation for wisdom preceded him and frankly, anyone was better than Maximian.

Ever the aesthetician, Constantine found Maximian's attempts at immortality impressive enough to leave many of them in place, especially the palace. The high walls Maximian placed around it could not hide the opulence of its grand baths and gardens; or the army of slaves who tended it. The grounds around it were extensive with dozens of auxiliary buildings and several fully staffed kitchens. The largest of these was at the rear of the primary residence. The two women working in it that autumn morning talked in whispers as they baked the morning bread and cleaned the kitchen.

"I don't care what you say, that man is more bloody-minded than Maximian ever was. I'm telling you, I saw it with my own eyes right outside this door," said Thalia, a handsome, middle-aged woman.

She laid aside her broom to point to a door leading to a courtyard and the stables. "They had him right out there. He was just a boy, tied up between two posts and they just ran him through with a hot blade over and again. 'Said he was a spy, but I doubt it. It was horrible to watch and the screaming – I can still hear it. Everyone says Constantine is the savior of the city. Humph! A foolish lie if ever I've heard one! He hides his dirt well. Dominus Maximian was at least truthful about it. If he executed someone everybody knew he did it and why."

"Ha! That's Ridiculous!" Her companion Ursa clucked. "What does it matter who the master kills, so long it's not you or me?"

Thalia glared at Ursa. They had this argument every couple of days. Thalia was Greek, practical in her ideas and a leftover from Maximian's days. She prided herself on loyalty to his house and she hated Constantine. While the rest of the city rejoiced in his arrival, Thalia knew the man for a murdering fraud.

Ursa, a round-faced, squat woman in her sixties stopped kneading her dough. She cast a wary eye over her shoulder. "–And it wasn't Constantine who ordered that boy killed, it was his wife. The dominus is a good man. I'd wager any amount he doesn't even know." As Ursa spoke, she added chunks of wood to the ceramic oven and peeked in at her loaves. They were just turning golden brown and filled the kitchen with a wonderful homely aroma.

Thalia laughed, she shook her head. "You're older, but I have lived among nobles much longer. I know things about them you don't. And I can tell you they keep honey smiles while they plunge knives in each other's backs. Constantine and his people are no different. The only decent soul in the lot is his son Crispus. Like night and day, those two. I suppose that is his mother's doing, I never saw Minervina before she died, but they say she was a gentle woman. And that she loved that boy to distraction. Constantine is hard and cruel but from that boy never so much as a harsh word."

"Too busy pulling serving girls into cupboards with him," Ursa snickered, running a blade down thick slices of an especially pungent cheese. She wrinkled her nose at the odor. "And the wenches don't complain about it either. Healthy boy and good-looking, who can blame them? I understand why the Domina notices him so when he comes to visit."

Thalia eased closer and lowered her voice. The conversation had only been dancing around trouble before; now it threatened to turn positively scandalous.

"What do you mean?" she whispered. "Are you saying there's something between the domina and her stepson that shouldn't be?" Although they were alone, Thalia glanced over her shoulder too. She grabbed the iron poker and scraped at the glowing embers as loudly as possible.

"I'm not saying that." Ursa put up a warning hand. "Not for his part at least. But the way that woman looks at him could melt hard wax, is all. She's not discrete about it in the least. I'm surprised you haven't noticed. I thought you knew everything that happened beneath this roof?"

Thalia laughed hard. "Oh, I don't doubt you. The domina has always been a nasty piece of work. Even when Fausta was a teenager, you should have seen how she behaved! Worse than a whore short on her rent! I think she and that body slave of hers must have bedded every senator and equestrian who came to visit. Sometimes together, I daresay. I was surprised that anybody married her, actually. I know her father had to offer her, but I still cannot believe Constantine took him up on it. He had to know.

Everybody has heard the stories about Fausta."

"Well, she has him now doesn't she?" Ursa rewrapped the remaining cheese and stowed it away in a cupboard. "And she and her girl Messalina still bed plenty of senators but you did not hear that from me. Messalina helps her keep it quiet and if Dominus wants to wear cuckold's horns it's no matter to anyone else," she said with amusement. "What Messalina should be keeping secret is how her mistress sniffs about after her stepson! Fausta has always been that kind of woman but as far as I know, Crispus has not given in to her advances."

Thalia chided her friend. "Shh that talk, even if true. I don't put it past her mind you, but Crispus is too decent and his father would surely kill him. It's Fausta. She transforms into a bitch in heat when fresh men are about. It's her best trick!"

The women laughed together in the bitter camaraderie birthed of mutual longings for a better life than the one they held. The women snatched their small satisfactions where they could and went back to work, baking the bread of the woman they ridiculed.

There was plenty to of work to do in the kitchens that day. The palace staff made ready a sumptuous feast for their emperor who played host to a talented group of men; senior members of the Senate, prominent civilian advisors and his most competent generals. They all made their way to Mediolanum for an important meeting.

The chamber where the counselors meet was larger than Constantius' war room in Eboracum with broad, vaulted ceilings, colorful frescos lining the walls, and small potted trees and ferns that overgrew their pots to spill their foliage unto black and white terrazzo floors. Dominating the center of the room was Constantine's exquisite cedar and granite desk, polished to a shine. Beautiful bear and tiger skin rugs were scattered on the floors to complement the arrangement. It was a masculine room, perfect for the war business inside its walls. The assembled men sat in backless chairs and on couches that made a wide circle around the desk.

In the years since Constantius died in Eboracum, the generals of Rome had been embroiled in a fight over his spoils. Constantine called the elite conclave to decide on a strategy to finish the bloody conflict at last and attendance by his best people was compulsory. Though some of the men had only just arrived from faraway places, they quickly assembled in Constantine's war room absent the baths and refreshment they craved after their journeys. While they waited for the emperor to join them, they discussed the events that had brought them there and enjoyed the efforts of the kitchen staff.

The loudest of the lot, Lucius Fulvius, was also the oldest man there, respected by all he had been a fierce fighter in his day. He had served under both Maximian and Constantine and before them, Diocletian. "Maxentius is a drunken, sex-addled buffoon but I have heard rumors that Maximian plans to rejoin him in Rome. Perhaps he has done it by now. Constantine should have killed that traitor long ago. And now his son is a plague on us as well. Mercy is too good for some."

Julius was quick to defend his commander and best friend. "What choice did he have? Fausta pleaded for her father's life and he could not abide her tears or her hatred if he forced patricide on her.

She was the one who revealed her father's plot."

The story had spread across the world, to every corner of the empire. Constantine's marriage to Maximian's daughter marked his ascent to Caesar of the West. The uneasy alliance helped legitimized Constantine in the Northern provinces and secured Rome and the rest of Italia for Maxentius, but from there the tale went awry. After enjoying the comforts of mother Rome, Maxentius was fat and happy. He soured on any aggression towards Constantine. Angered by his refusal, Maximian raised a coup against his son. It was close, but Maxentius managed to keep the soldiers on his side by draining the Capitoline treasury and promising them even more if they captured his father for him.

Ironically, with his plan foiled and his own son calling for his head, Maximian had to flee to his daughter and Constantine. When he tried the same low trick with them, stealing Constantine's men and proclaiming himself emperor again, Fausta betrayed the scheme to her husband. Constantine beat back the ill-advised attempt to usurp him and after that, relations soured between the two families for good. Most of those who dared whisper about the matter felt as Lucius Fulvius, that Constantine should have killed the man for the insult.

Gallus Cincius, a fat senator from the East with questionable loyalties spoke up next. "Be careful with calling men traitors. With so many changing alliances, everyone might be at some point or another. Galerius is Augustus in the East, Licinius, in the West and Maximian Daia and Constantine are Caesars. The tetrarchy has been working for decades. Now we have this great hoo-ha with everyone and his uncle staking his claim. Everything relies on the alliances Constantine makes now. I count myself one of his friends and it is no secret where I once stood. Galerius is my kinsman, but here I sit on the side of Constantine. People can change, Fulvius."

"You defend traitors now?" Lucius Fulvius spat out. "Next, you will tell me Licinius is a friend instead of a schemer. Should Constantine make an alliance with him too? And all this while Maximian licks his chops in the background. Mark me, we have not heard the last of that old demon. Maximian is our chief concern, I tell you!"

A heavy-browed and swarthy complexioned man wearing the red-striped toga of a senator added, "And why not make alliances? Why not band with Licinius? He's bound by blood to the general and Licinius is no friend to Maximian."

Though there were general murmurs of distain, no one really raised a protest to the idea.

"Maybe your primary concern in this is Maximian and wishing the man dead but my concerns are far removed from yours. I simply want to finish this thing however we can so that we can all go home." Valerius Maximus Basilius cut in. He adjusted his toga on his muscular frame with a self-important shrug. He was an important senator, a *populare*[6] and a man aligned with Constantine's house since days unknown. "My loyalty has never been in question, so if that is what this is all about, I'll take my leave. I need a bath at any rate." He rose to leave, fairly dripping with arrogance.

---

[6] Political party which favored the common people, opposed by the Optimates, the party favored by the nobility

"No one is going anywhere. You dogs will do your duty, or deal with me." Julius said. His hand near his sword was an open if unnecessary threat. Basilius sank back into his seat with a sheepish grin that usually charmed but failed this time.

The conversation would have delved even deeper into politics and the infighting that comes with it, but the arrival of the emperor stilled their tongues. Constantine strolled through the scarlet curtains with the same noble military bearing his father possessed. The emperor stood before the assembled men alert and stony-faced.

"Thank you gentlemen for meeting me here. Some of you have come from far places. Don't think I don't appreciate your commitment to our cause." He stopped to smile here at the unspoken irony since fear of his wrath was the real motivator for many of them.

"Three years ago my father gave me a charge, to see Rome cleansed of her enemies both within and without. Today we are here to answer a threat. I would see the men who call themselves Romans, who have been holding our lands captive in their greedy hands, laid low. You are here to help me find the best way to do that. We must end these conflicts that serve no purpose save to make us vulnerable to attacks from outside our borders where the true enemy lurks, waiting for us to kill each other." He stopped then and turned even more serious. "What then is the word of my counselors on these matters?" And he waited for it to begin.

Some necessary administrative issues occupied the first minutes. Grain rations, legionnaire pay, how to secure more bribes from begging satraps looking for Roman favors, but then they turned to the real challenge.

Lucius Fulvius again spoke up, "We are facing a beast of our own making. The Roman war machine is a thousand years old. Our mastery is threatened only by our countrymen. When our legions fight each other, the result is always a slaughter and being the better commander is no guarantee." He stopped here to give Constantine a pointed look. "There have been a few exceptions, Julius Caesar at Pharsalus[7] for one, but the general with the most men, healthy and able to fight usually wins when Romans fight each other."

So where do we stand in that regard?" Constantine demanded to know.

Senator Bassianus, betrothed to Constantine's sister Anastasia, and Constantine's newly appointed Dux[8], spoke up. Tasked by Constantine with calculating fighting strength, he was middle-aged and handsome if not particularly bright. He fumbled with a few scraps of parchment, and then gave his report. "We have 35,000 infantry and 5,000 cavalry, far short of the number we need. Marching on the south seems ill-advised unless we swell our ranks before the spring, which will be difficult. For the time being, we must choose – either you challenge Maxentius for Rome, or you hold the Rhine border against the Germanic tribes. You cannot do both."

Fulvius was a valued member of Constantine's Evocati Augusti, an invitation-only college of high-ranking veterans bonded into fresh service. He

---

[7] Decisive victory during Caesar's civil war against Pompey Magnus over control of Rome.
[8] Military chief commanding troops in the provinces, answering only to the senior general.

cleared his throat with a loud rattle. "He's correct. Holding the frontiers is more than a notion. The treasury cannot sustain the cost of a campaign south any time soon. Those resources are better spent elsewhere, I think. Maxentius is well caught in Rome. He cannot venture far north so there is no immediate need to oppose him. We should concentrate on the borders and leave Rome to Maxentius."

The other assembled men stared at Fulvius.

"You coward! What kind of sniveling answer is that?" Julius asked him. Contempt dripped from each word. Fulvius turned cold eyes on him and began rising from his couch, slowly given his age, but rising nonetheless. His trembling hands were curled into fists that scared no one. Julius stood as well, though he did not bother to clench his fists at the old man.

Constantine broke in to quell the squabble. "Peace gentlemen! Keep to the matters at hand. How many cities with stocked treasuries between here and Rome? Our attacks on them will secure more than enough gold to train and pay more men and we'll gather strength as we go."

"That's all well and good sir, but there are only one or two that fit that description," said Pacatianus, a fox-faced prefect for the military's treasury, the *aerarii militaris*. "I made quiet inquiries as you commanded. Maxentius has 90,000 men-at-arms now, his ranks enlarged by men deserting Galerius and Severus."

Constantine spoke. "Those legions were under my father at one time and their loyalty is divided at best. I shall exploit that. Maxentius is not as popular as one might think. His support erodes by the hour. The people grow tired of seeing their friends and neighbors butchered like cattle over religion, and of his building projects bleeding them of every coin. When the cities of Italia open to us, willingly, we will increase our ranks to a size that will more than match whatever troops he has managed to cobble together."

As he spoke, he paced the room with a restless energy the others pretended did not unnerve them. Constantine stopped before a bust of Aurelian. He let his hand rest against the base for a moment. Aurelian was an exceptional emperor, but that was no bother to his own Praetorians when they murdered him.

The mantle of power was a heavy burden Constantine was just beginning to understand. It was a rare species of insanity that invited men to heap such troubles on their heads. The image of Constantius, as he passed the imperial signet ring to him, filled his mind. His father thought him worthy and his father was a wise man. And that wisdom emboldened Constantine to resist the doubts that lingered. He turned to face the group again.

"So we will go south?" Julius said, reading his expression. He rubbed his hands together as though they itched to feel a sword clutched between them again. "As long as there is the risk of life and limb involved, I'm ready," he laughed.

"Yes, we move south, but *caveat viator*[9] Julius," Constantine said patiently. "This is no time for reckless advances. We must choose our targets with care. We want news of our approach spreading to good effect. Then people will see the wisdom in

---

[9] Latin, meaning traveler beware

welcoming us into their gates."

"South? So the people embrace us as liberators…unlikely but possible I grant you, but what of our northern borders? We cannot forget them. I'm afraid that if Germania is lost, we are lost with her." Bassianus said, earning him a frown from Constantine. He walked over to glare down at him. Bassianus suddenly looked very small in his chair.

"You sound like a woman!"

Some of the arrogance left Bassianus' eyes, he blanched and fell silent.

Pride spread across Constantine's face. "My son Crispus has done well on the frontier. He has held my rule this long; I have no doubt he will continue to do so." The emperor's eagle-eyed gaze swept the room; none were foolish enough to disagree. No one even moved, except Julius, who leaned forward to grab a few olives from a nearby bowl.

When he spoke, it was around a mouthful of them. "Crispus has done extraordinary work. You should reward him. Some honor worthy of his acclaim." A few pieces of the olives flew from his mouth and landed on Bassianus' arm. Angry and disgusted, he brushed them away. Julius popped a few more olives into his mouth and laughed while Bassianus seethed.

Constantine's smile was unusually dry and tight. "I would not go so far as to call it acclaim, Julius. He is but a reflection of the strength in our blood."

Julius nodded. "True but he has done better than most, certainly better than I did at his age." In a rare display of discretion, Julius left unsaid that perhaps Crispus was better than Constantine too.

"Just as I had to earn my accolades so shall he," Constantine said. "If Crispus continues to show his worth, I will name him my Praetorian Prefect—" Julius looked up in surprise, nearly choking on his olives. "—And since he is, in fact, already governing Germania, I shall have him named Proconsul as well. As a proconsul, he can levy his own troops to defend the border." Constantine waited while Julius recovered with a healthy swig of wine.

"This surprises you Julius? You just sung the boy's praises. I didn't know you cared so much for a title, you old goat. You belong in the thick of things, Julius, not hovering over me as Praetorian. This could be your last war season; you want to make a good showing of it, don't you?"

Julius turned the thought over in his mind for a moment, then shrugged. "Why should I care? Battles are won with swords not titles. I never thought it suited me anyway, but Constantius insisted. I'll gladly step aside if you want to give the headache to Crispus instead." Julius went back to his wine and olives with a loud belch. He raised an eyebrow. "You're not planning on cutting my pay, are you?" he asked only half-mocking.

Constantine chuckled, "Of course not, why deprive the wenches loitering about your chambers of their profits?" Julius laughed with him and Constantine slapped him on the back. "It is settled then. Crispus will hold the Rhine while I move south. And as the reward for his services to the state, I will have him ratified as Proconsul of Germania in the Senate. . . As soon as I boot Maxentius from it!"

The room erupted in applause from some of

the more gratuitous sycophants. It died away abruptly when Constantine ignored it. There was an awkward pause then a snigger, from Julius as usual.

Constantine said, "The feast of Meditrinalia provides the perfect opportunity to make the announcement. Couriers have already been dispatched to summon Crispus to the celebration."

A few of the senators expressed concerns. "That's only a few weeks away…premature…he's still a boy…" Their murmurs filled the room like tiny bees and carried as much of a sting.

Constantine swatted at the air in annoyance. "Quiet! It will be as I say." And that ended that. The only sounds were the servants moving about taking away empty platters and refilling wine cups while Constantine changed the subject. He began a discussion of which legions would move south and which would stay put in Germania for the time being.

The hour grew late. The braziers and wall torches were lit while Constantine and company settled into their drinks in earnest. Their discussions became irreverent, focusing on women, wild times and old victories. A harpist played somewhere and the sounds of the household settling down for the evening filled the palace. Tinkling laughter drifted in from the peristyle where the emperor's young daughters, Constantina and Helena toddled indiscriminately about the greenery, their frustrated nursemaids in hard pursuit of the busy little girls. In the kitchen, the ovens kept the sweetmeats and desserts warm and ready for the guests. And along the perimeter of the gardens, servants swept the tiled floors oblivious to a female figure standing half-hidden in the shadows of one of the marble columns.

The woman slipped quietly back along the colonnade, to the suite of rooms dedicated to Empress Fausta. She ran lightly, her feet scarcely touching the pathway. Her stola was a lovely shade of midnight blue made from fine Tamilian cotton; it whipped about just above her manicured toes. She was Messalina, the empress' voluptuous body slave and her devoted confidant. Messalina was an exquisite beauty, but also uncommonly intelligent with a remarkable memory for details, something Fausta exploited whenever she could.

When Fausta asked her to report on Constantine's war meeting, she had been happy to comply. Now with her task completed, she could not reach her mistress fast enough to spill everything she had heard.

Chapter Four:

Sister's Keeper

Inside Fausta's candlelit rooms, the empress was surrounded by servants scurrying to and fro to prepare her for bed. After a long soak in her private caldarium[10], she reclined on a couch, refreshed and happy. A light robe loosely covered her body and an attendant massaged her legs and feet. A small, half drank cup of mulsum[11] boiled with cinnamon and laurel sat beside her on the dressing table. She yawned, already feeling the effects of it. Her silky-haired Maltese pup lay curled up on her lap, occasionally growling at the servants if they ventured too close. The pup's name was Issa and she was a haughty little bitch, prone to sharp bites when she did not get her way. Conversely, she and her mistress got along quite well; the slaves whispered it was because nobody else could stand either of them.

Without warning, Messalina entered the room in a rush of flying skirts and flowing hair. She hurried to Fausta's side to whisper in her ear. Fausta listened with quiet interest. She dismissed the slaves around her, including the one massaging her, and dropped

---

[10] The hot water chamber of a three room Roman bath.
[11] Wine mixed with honey

her beloved Issa to the floor. Unhappy to find herself so rudely displaced, Issa growled at Messalina as she scampered off to the sheepskin rug beneath Fausta's bed. She crouched there, baring her teeth around her favorite bone as though it were Messalina's leg. Messalina ignored the little pest. She sat down beside her mistress and immediately spilled the secrets she overheard from the war council.

"First, Domina, someone mentioned your father. The word is Maximian's escaped Constantine's custody and is on his way to rejoin your brother in Rome." Fausta drew a sharp breath but said nothing, allowing Messalina to continue. "It seems your husband now wishes that he had killed Maximian after what happened in Massilia, and avoided all this trouble with him and your brother."

Fausta nodded, "Well, I can't say I blame him, though he probably blames me for talking him out of it. As though I had a choice in the matter. Maximian is my father! Of course, I urged Constantine to be merciful! My father is still furious with me for telling Constantine at all. He and my brother should be grateful. If he is now able to join Maxentius, it will be by my hand that kept him alive and able to do so."

"Domina, forgive me, but that's the point. I don't think your father is safe at all. I heard talk of a forced suicide and the emperor will demand it if they capture him again."

Fausta sighed in resignation. "There's nothing I can do if that happens. I cannot risk coming to the rescue again for my father, or my brother. I shall never have peace for constantly needing to save one or the other of them. Their scheming is incessant and always comes to a bad end."

Messalina usually kept quiet when it came to the men of the family. Her relationships with Fausta's father and brother were complicated. "I have other news, Domina. Though, you will like it even less. The emperor plans to name Crispus to Pretorian Prefect. He plans to give him Germania when he moves south against your brother. The announcement will come during the wine festival. A summons had already gone to Treverorum."

"Eh, how is that? Julius is the Prefect. I cannot believe that brute would allow himself to be usurped."

"He did allow it – took it as good news even."

"That rat Crispus as chief among the men keeping Constantine alive and holding imperium in Germania? The boy will have an open path to take anything he wants, including his father's life. Constantine is a fool if he does not see his son for what he is!"

Fausta pounded her fists against the couch in frustration. Her brow furrowed and she disappeared into her troubled thoughts. She rose and walked to the narrow terrace outside her rooms to watch the sun disappearing over the palace walls. Messalina watched with growing concern as Fausta stood in profile against the approaching night. Knowing her mistress loved the smell, she commanded the servants to light incense throughout the chamber. A strong fragrance of bergamot and vanilla wafted out to soothe Fausta as she watched the sky turn ever-deepening shades of violet.

As the empress stood on her balcony surrounded by the calming scents, she refocused her energy, puzzling out ways to answer the very real threat her stepson posed to her and her children. At last she spoke her thoughts.

"I must be quick about this. I would not have Crispus take a place so close to his father. Constantine never even married that foreign whore who bore him. I am his lawful wife and my children should – no, will follow him!" Her need to protect her children gave her courage. Her political and social shrewdness came from years of keeping two paces ahead of everyone around her. The answer to this threat was lurking somewhere and she would find it.

Messalina waited patiently on the couch for her mistress to reveal her plan. The night was full on when Fausta finally turned away from the lovely sight of the Palatine hill and the city below it laid out before her. The soft glow of the candles and wall torches provided flickering light and at Fausta's request, Messalina joined her on the balcony. Now that evening had arrived, the heavens blazed forth with a million stars. As Fausta and Messalina watched, a single point of light streaked across the sky, leaving a fiery trail behind it. They took it for a favorable sign that the gods were watching over them.

"Domina," Messalina touched Fausta's hand. Their eyes met in unspoken agreement and they slid closer together on the balcony, their arms encircling each other. "Whatever you have decided is blessed by the gods. I know it must be dangerous because you hesitate in telling me your plans, but I promise you I will not fail you if you let me help."

"You have never failed me Messalina. We will see this boy to his end…and the gods will light the path for us."

"And you shall see your fortunes rise, as they

always have when you do what the timid will not."

Fausta laughed, the sound was full and rich. "I'm not sure that's a good thing." Messalina joined her and the bond they shared reassured them both.

Standing in the dim light from Fausta's bedchamber, the women were striking to behold in very different ways. Fausta was tall, graceful and more wickedly beautiful than any decent woman should be. She had a mane of dark brown hair that fell in tumbling waves down her back and wide, jade-green eyes set into a heart-shaped face. Her skin was a warm, sun-kissed color in keeping with her Illyrian heritage. She had a figure to bring Venus to envy. The soft curves visible under her stola and her full breasts never failed to leave men enraptured, most especially her husband. Constantine was entirely infatuated with her, a fact that had never failed to work in her favor.

Then there was Messalina, at twenty-eight she was a mere two years Fausta's junior and equally stunning. She was as tall and shapely as her mistress, with deep auburn hair that caressed her face and shoulders. Her eyes were the color of storm clouds, deep gray with a hint of purple and beautifully mysterious. Framed by her naturally arched brows and refined bone structure; they perfectly complimented her full lips and relaxed smile. She was a rare creature with a touch of the exotic about her. Men adored her beauty and enjoyed her body with equal relish; yet she loved no one except Fausta.

"You and I have been through difficult times before, eh?" Fausta whispered to her. "I do have a plan but I'll need you by my side."

Messalina nodded. "I'll do whatever you ask."

It had always been so between them, since the

time Messalina arrived in the imperial household at the tender age of eight. Maximian chose her himself during an afternoon visit to the most fashionable market in Rome, the Saepta Julia. His wife, the Empress Europa had died of a sudden illness and Fausta had been beyond comforting. Maximian gladly paid the outrageous price of 4000 denarii for the Thracian beauty that would be his daughter's body slave and playmate in the wake of her mother's death. The girls became inseparable as they grew up together in the imperial household. There was a genuine love between them that went beyond slave and mistress. They grew lovelier and more confident with each passing year, until misfortune found them.

Messalina was twelve and Fausta fourteen when they discovered the true reason for Messalina's presence in the household and why such a high price was paid for her beauty.

One night Maximian came for the girl, rousing her out of a deep sleep. He took her roughly without concern for her age or inexperience. When he was done with her, it was only a few moments before Maxentius took his turn. Messalina endured them in shocked, terrified silence save for muffled sobs. She ran to Fausta as soon as they left her, her terror and pain forgotten in her fear that Fausta had been equally mistreated. When she found Fausta asleep untouched and safe, she was afraid to speak of her shame. She had never felt her captivity as a weight around her neck until then; as she stood shaking and bloody in Fausta's rooms while the noble girl slept peacefully.

Once Fausta coaxed the tear-soaked truth from Messalina, she was livid. She rushed to confront her father and brother. She heaped insults upon their heads, screamed and cried herself sick, but they refused to give up their prize. To silence Fausta though, they promised kindness and rewards for her obedience. Messalina tried to be satisfied; the other slaves, who received no such accommodation, told her she was lucky. Out of love, Messalina turned the gifts and coins they gave her over to Fausta, who saved them so they could one day run away together. Such were the dreams of little girls growing up with the realities of what it meant to be women. The girls matured, and as both took lovers, they perfected their use of guile and seduction. And so, their corruption was complete. Every man Fausta or Messalina took to bed had a purpose for being there, whether he knew it or not.

The escape plan never came to fruition, and eventually Fausta returned the gifts and money Messalina entrusted to her over the years. The occasion presented Messalina the opportunity to buy her freedom, but she refused be parted from her mistress. Fausta was happy to accept her devotion. She was lost without Messalina, and so they persevered together in a world full of dangerous people, where murder and betrayal were everyday occurrences.

Now, as they watched the stars and listened to the night cicadas, Fausta laid out her newly hatched scheme in intricate detail. Messalina hung on every word. Once she was finished, Fausta went back inside to her desk. She wrote a short letter, stamped it with her personal seal and held it out to Messalina.

"Make certain this reaches my brother. If we fail, I may need his protection. Send someone you trust. Both our lives will depend on it." Failure meant discovery as traitors, but if Crispus did not fall, she was sure Constantine would at his hand and Fausta and her children would be next.

Messalina was confident as always. "I will see to it, Domina. Don't fret. Your brother will get the message."

"And make sure whomever you send places it directly into his hand and no other."

"As you say, Domina." Messalina took the scrap of vellum and left quickly for the garrison just beyond the city. She had many love-struck admirers among the soldiers there, willing to do her bidding for a chance to get closer to her. The trick was finding the right one.

Fausta watched her go, and then turned her face heavenward. She clasped her hands to her breasts and prayed to the only other person she trusted. "Mother, if you can hear me, ask the gods to favor my plans. Please!"

Chapter Five:

Unexpected News

Augusta Treverorum, September 309

Augusta Treverorum, an old, well-established city, lay nestled in a curved expanse of the Moselle River Valley in the province of Gallia. The city was a favorite of Constantius Chlorus, long before he made it his capital. The emperor worked many years to repair the devastation and rot brought on by the many foreign attacks on the city. After his father's death, Constantine continued the work then left Crispus in command of their pet project. To protect it, Crispus surrounded the city with high walls and gates, the largest of which was the Porte Nigra that marked the northern boundary.

On this particular morning, a cold wind blew in endless gales, and the heavens dumped needle-sharp rain on already drenched streets. Despite heavy cloaks and the shelter of the gatehouse, the men guarding the Porta Nigra were miserable. As they shivered and talked to keep warm, they were surprised to see a full retinue of horsemen advance slowly on the gate, battling against the pounding rains.

As the riders closed the distance, their red cloaks marked them as legionaries. Noting the leather satchel at the leader's side, the guards snapped to attention. Imperial messengers were a rarity in Treverorum. "What fresh hell is this I wonder," mumbled a young tribune under his breath. He ran off to fetch someone superior enough to receive the visitors.

By the time the horsemen reached the gate, Marcius, a seasoned Praetorian whom Crispus trusted above all others, had been rousted from his meal. He awaited the unexpected visitors with a surly expression at the interruption to his venison stew.

"State your business." Marcius eyed the group with suspicion. The men were haggard and soaked through from the rains. They had ridden their horses to exhaustion; the animals stood with drooped heads and spirits. One had even fallen to its knees, dumping its rider to the wet ground where he lay motionless, as tired as his horse.

What could be so important that they nearly killed themselves and their beasts to get here? Marcius thought. He watched as the leader rooted through his satchel and emerged with a crumpled piece of parchment clutched in his fist.

"We have orders to deliver a message to Legatus Crispus and to return to Mediolanum immediately with his answer. And we will need fresh mounts. As you can see, ours are too worn out to go on."

"I would say that's an understatement. Dead is more like it!" one of the gate guards sniggered. Marcius turned to his men, searching in vain for the one bold enough to embarrass him in front of strangers. Unable to find the guilty party, a red-faced Marcius gave orders to the gatekeepers who were huddled together, looking anywhere but at him. "Right then, don't just stand there like deaf-mutes! Tend to their horses and find them some dry clothes!" He directed the travelers to the watchtower where they could dry themselves, then snatched the note from the leader. He headed to the praetorium where the Legatus made his private quarters.

The praetorium was an unadorned limestone and granite building that extended some twenty-five feet in each direction along the back wall of the castra. Marcius strode quickly inside. He paused to rebuke the loafing soldier who was meant to guard the door but was leaning against the wall daydreaming instead. Inside, he found the Legatus. Crispus was sprawled haphazardly across a couch, in the midst of a nap.

He slept fitfully, his body twitching at times under the thick wool blanket that wound around him. His gladius[12] lay by his side and even in sleep, his body was as taut as a plucked arrow. His usually clean-shaven face was edged in a sparse beard that revealed his young age. His thick, dark brown curls were streaked with the black soil of the river valley, a left over from a skirmish the night before. The battle clung stubbornly to him, under his nails and on the bloodstained tunic he wore. His handsome features were marked by exhaustion, and his eyes, big, round moons like his father, were ringed with dark circles.

Crispus and his men had beaten back yet

---

[12] A two edged sword, broad and of equal width from hilt to point, it was used by soldiers and gladiators.

another raid on the garrison, from the Franks this
time. The small, hostile tribes surrounding
Treverorum never allowed the people to live in peace
for very long. Every few weeks, one or another of
them would attack, and it seemed that no matter how
many were killed, more always returned.

Marcius had entered the room quietly, not
wanting to startle his commander, but Crispus was
instantly alert to his presence.

He opened his eyes and murmured. "Yes,
Marcius, what is it?"

"A courier just arrived with an urgent
message for you." Marcius laid the note on the couch
beside him.

Crispus sat up slowly, shaking off sleep. He
picked up the rolled piece of parchment. "Urgent,
eh?" He scanned the crumpled sheet. "This is just a
summons to attend the wine festival in a fortnight."
He laid the note aside and stood to his feet, easily
towering over his soldier.

Marcius continued, "The courier arrived with
a full envoy of armed guards. They rode without rest
to get here and they have orders to escort you to
Mediolanum immediately."

"Indeed. Well, I suppose I must go then."
Crispus said, puzzled by all of it. He called for writing
material, dashed off a few lines, then handed the
finished parchment to Marcius. "Give these directives
to the quartermaster and see to the travel
arrangements. I'll leave today and you shall come with
me. It will be good to get away from this fighting for
a bit eh?" Marcius nodded sharply and left him,
visibly excited for an adventure outside the castra.

Later, Crispus sat alone, his mind turning in

circles, all coming back to one central point. Why the rush? Attending the Meditrinalia festival was no urgent matter. It was too much to hope, but perhaps his father had good reason for wanting him back. Was it too late in the year to plan a triumph for him? In his solitude, his musings didn't feel so absurd. He held together a factious province by the force of his will and had accumulated a respectable list of victories. Were they enough to finally convince his father he was worthy of him?

Crispus rested on his couch and let his imagination run free. In his mind, a vision unfurled of him in Rome with marching soldiers and cheering crowds all screaming his name, the air around him thick with rose petals. Wreaths of oak leaves were looped and tossed around everything in sight. He saw the best of the nobility seated in ranks at the end of the Via Sacra while his father and stepmother waited for him nearby on a raised dais. He imagined them sitting on gold inlaid chairs with an empty seat between them, reserved for him. The whole city had turned out for the occasion – all to honor him. Crispus could almost taste the wine that would flow and the glory that would be his. Most of all, he tried to envision his father's face, proud of him at last. It was a futile endeavor. Constantine's face swam enticingly out of focus each time he tried to imagine it.

"Well," he said, as if to dispel the fantasy, "there is only one way to find out what he wants, and that is to go." He stood up in one fluid movement and headed to the stables to check on Viatoro, his Nisean stallion.

When Crispus walked into the stable; the

horse sensed him immediately. He stamped on the ground in his stall. After months of boarding with only short runs to exercise him, Viatoro was more than ready for some action. Crispus rarely rode him into battle, valuing the horse too much to risk him taking an arrow meant for him. Viatoro jerked his head and shifted about until Crispus calmed him with steady strokes on his back and whispers in his ear.

"I know you're tired of this place – me too. How about we get out of here for a while and have some fun?" Viatoro's soft neighing was all the answer he needed. He patted the horse and fed him an apple grabbed from a nearby basket.

The stallion was nothing short of magnificent. After generations of breeding in the royal houses of Persia, the Nisean treasure horses were the most prized in the world. Crispus had the rare privilege of having owned two of the finest, Viatoro and his mother, Viatora. The horses had particular significance to him as the last gifts from his mother who died so long ago.

As he stroked Viatoro's coat, he wished with all his heart he could talk to his mother. Minervina was the only person who could have helped him make sense of his feelings about his father. Crispus had seen very little of Constantine while his mother lived; he was always away fighting wars or dodging assassination plots. The only thing he remembered about his father from that time was that he never smiled, and was always vexed about something. His parents were rarely together, and when they were, they were not very happy.

He vividly remembered the day his mother called him to her bedside at their home in Bithynia.

Crispus was eight years old at the time, and they were living in a large villa near Nicomedia, the capital. His mother had been ill for months, and the servants had to prop her up on her sickbed so she could speak to him. He thought of how weak she had been that cold morning, so like this one. Her arms were as pale and thin as the bones within them when she reached out to pull him close to her. He hugged her, and she seemed to grow smaller in his arms. Instead of her usual sweet scent of jasmine, there was a salty, slightly rancid odor about her. He remembered sadly the sound of her voice as she whispered to him. It was soft and raspy, and it caught several times as she tried to make him understand what was about to happen to both of them. She explained to him that it was time for him to leave her to be with his father in Gallia.

The adult Crispus was ashamed of his childish reaction. He had been petulant, whining to her. "But why? You have been sick before and you have always gotten better. Why are you sending me away now? You don't love me anymore!" He regretted the words as soon as he said them. Her eyes filled with tears. She pushed him back and grasped his tiny hands in hers. He knew she was trying to be strong, but her eyes told a different story.

He did not understand the fear he saw in them, so he did the only thing he could do. He continued pleading with her. With the natural selfishness of a child, he focused his attention on what he needed, and paid no heed to her pain.

She stopped him with a finger to his lips. "Crispus, my lamb, listen to me now. I am dying, son. I'm sorry. I wish I could stay with you, but it is happening. I have to know that you are safe before I go. Please understand." Now she was the pleading one. "Your father has too many enemies for you to stay here. You must leave and go where he can protect you."

"But I don't even know him! He doesn't like me. Please don't make me go. You're not dying! You'll make it through, just like all the other times, but then I'll be gone and you'll be all alone!" Crispus jumped up from the bed and stomped his feet. He did not want to have a tantrum, but he could not help it. He was eight years old, hurt, scared, and all he wanted was for his mother to hold him in her arms and tell him everything would be all right.

"I won't go! Say I don't have to go. Mother, please!"

Minervina was patient. "This time is different. Promise me, you will be a good boy for your father. He loves you, and you will come to know it one day." She smiled and held him while he cried.

That conversation was the last he would have with his mother this side of eternity. He left for Gallia at first light the next day. Two months later, she was dead.

His Aunt Zenobia and her husband Boteiras, came from Nicomedia to deliver the terrible news. Crispus was sitting with a few of the men outside the praetorium when his father approached with them beside him. Crispus had known instantly that his mother was gone. A cold, black emptiness rose in his chest and lingered even now within him.

"Aunt Zenobia, my mother..." he had said, but his voice caught in his throat and water welled in his eyes. He looked up at his father. Constantine's hard gaze in the face of his grief pierced him and made Crispus swallow his words, and his tears. It was on that terrible day that he inherited Viatora from his mother. She was the height of a man with a child on his shoulders, with a golden brown coat and a luxurious jet-black mane. Her eyes were bright brown and intelligent. She was the granddaughter of a beloved mare his mother and aunt hand-raised back in their Armenian homeland when they were children.

Beginning that day, Crispus spent most of his time in the stables, taking care of the mare and pouring all the love he felt for his mother onto her. When the time came, he mated her to another Nisean. She gave birth to a single foal, a male the color of spun gold. Crispus named him Viatoro, and they had been inseparable ever since. Now they would head to Mediolanum and a better fate, he hoped.

Crispus was more relaxed after his visit with Viatoro. He went back to his private study to read his beloved Greek tragedies while his travel arrangements were made. Hours passed as he lost himself in *The Suppliants* and *Antigone*, two his mother used to read to him, hoping their political ideas, and life lessons on honor and devotion would take root within him. He could not say that it was so, but they offered him some comfort now as he prepared to see his father.

Mediolanum was a two-week journey from Treverorum, but they could be there in ten days, weather permitting and with no brigands to kill on the way. They left the garrison in the mid-afternoon. The horses clopped along in an ageless rhythm joined by the tinkling sound of metal on metal as the men's weapons bumped against their saddle horns. The sound dulled Crispus' senses. To stay awake, he began to think about the one person he truly wanted to see during his visit, his friend Julia, though it was unlikely they would be able to see one another.

Julia was the youngest daughter of Augustus Galerius. Crispus had met her in Nicomedia when she was seven and he was ten. He was in Bithynia for the summer to visit his Grandmother Helena, his first visit there since his mother's death. He and Julia had become fast friends or perhaps something more, but he had not seen her in years. The last time they saw each other it had not gone well. He wondered if she was still angry with him. If she were, he could not say he blamed her.

He put it aside though. It was more frustrating to think of her than to contemplate what his father wanted with him. "I don't suppose it matters much right now. Let's just enjoy the journey, eh 'Toro?" He patted the horse's head. It was time he saw his father again, whatever the reason for the summons.

Chapter Six

The Baths of Hercules

Nine days later Crispus and his riders sighted Mediolanum in the distance. Word of his impending arrival had begun appearing quietly in the Acta Diurna[13] three days prior. Whispers turned to confirmation and now that he was close, the news spread like unchecked fire. As soon as Crispus and his men appeared at the Porta Nova, the first entry point to the city, happy crowds lining the roadway mobbed them, hoping to catch a glimpse of the emperor's heroic, illegitimate son. What should have been a short ride turned into a two-hour odyssey of hugs, handshakes, pats on the back and the occasional grope.

"You would think they have never seen soldiers returning home before now!" Crispus grumbled. It rang false however, in light of the grin on his face.

Marcius did not hear a word of it. Right then he was preoccupied with disengaging his leg from an overenthusiastic prostitute. She had an unusually firm

---

[13] A kind of gazette published daily under the authority of the Roman government, placed in the forum it held general news and announcements.

grip on him and ran alongside his horse. She promised all manner of services in the lewdest terms possible.

"Later, woman!" he laughed. "Wait for me outside the palace!" He managed to shake free of her, only to find others wrestling to take her place.

"She-wolves," Marcius spurred his horse forward before any other marauding vagrants could grab hold of him.

"They won't leave you alone huh? You are supposed to protect me Marcius, not the other way around!" Crispus said with a laugh when he caught up with his bodyguard after shaking off his own stragglers.

The streets pulsed with milling crowds of careworn peasants, finely dressed nobles, and all manner of tradesmen. The noise was tremendous, but when Crispus reached the palace there was no sign anyone noticed the fuss. In fact, no one noticed anything at all, the yards were empty. Crispus pulled up Viatoro's reins and slowed at the still-locked iron gates. Several minutes passed. When it became apparent no one was coming outside to greet the returning hero, the crowds began to wander off. As they went away, Crispus heard derisive whispers and chuckles behind him. His grin faded at the corners. He kept it in place for the sake of his men, but his embarrassment was keen.

"Marcius, go and find someone to open the damn gate!" he commanded sharply.

It was an unnecessary order. Marcius had slid to the ground when he was sure no one was coming to welcome them. He was already heading to the rear of the palace to look for an attendant. After another eternity, which saw the few remaining loiterers give up and leave, the front doors were thrown open. The Imperial Steward, Atticus descended the stone steps and hobbled to the gate as quickly as his ancient legs could carry him.

"Young Dominus! I'm so sorry! We were not expecting you for several days yet. Please my lord, come inside!" He called behind him to someone yet unseen. "Rufus! Where are you, boy?"

Atticus fumbled with the gate locks, his gnarled fingers made clumsier by age and bad nerves. While he loosed the heavy chain, a breathless youth ran up to him. Bits of straw littered his hair, and his tunic hung off one shoulder. He tried to straighten it in vain; it remained as limp and dull as the boy himself.

Atticus attacked immediately. "Imbecillus! You're supposed to watch the gate. I'll beat you within an inch of your life! See to their horses and be quick about it!" He slapped the boy roughly about the head and pushed him through the gate. Rufus stumbled under the blow but managed to right himself. He ran to take Viatoro's reins from Crispus.

"Be calm. It's no matter," Crispus insisted. He patted Viatoro lightly on the head before handing him over to Rufus. "Where is my father?"

Eager to redeem himself, the old man beamed at them, exposing a nearly toothless grin. "The emperor is resting in the exhedra[14] with the empress. Please Dominus..." he stepped aside and swept an arm toward the palace, "Come with me. I'll inform

---

[14] A large, elegant room usually located at the rear of a Roman villa, it usually led outside to a rear courtyard.

them you have arrived."

"Very well," Crispus said, though he frowned at the mention of his stepmother. He turned to Marcius who was nearby now, awaiting orders. "The men are dismissed until after the feast." He tossed him a heavy bag of coins. "Here – go enjoy yourself. I will see you in a few days' time."

Marcius caught the bag, surprise spreading across his face. "Thank you, sir. I'll put it to good use!" He laughed, before disappearing with a mischievous glint in his eye.

Crispus went through the gates into the main domus. The vestibule of the palace was exquisite; no expense was spared during its renovations. The vaulted ceilings rose fifteen feet into the air and were covered with brightly painted frescoes and mosaics depicting historical scenes from the glorious early days of the Roman Republic. The walls were decorated with detailed landscapes of Greek temples and scenes from nature in the ancient second style, now in fashion again. Every few feet there stood pale marble busts of the former emperors and tall, ornately crafted columns. The floor was designed in beautiful alternating squares of priceless ivory and obsidian.

Atticus left Crispus in the vestibule after ensuring he was ensconced with wine and food and rushed away into the recesses of the palace. Shortly afterward the emperor himself appeared with Empress Fausta trailing behind him. They surprised Crispus who was devouring a bowl of hard-cooked eggs as though they were his last meal. He swallowed quickly and stood to face them.

"Father! I –" he managed before Constantine interrupted him.

"My son, you appear as a spirit without warning!" Crispus noticed a glimmer of approval in his eyes. Constantine embraced him. "How did you get here so quickly? You were not expected until the Ides at the earliest."

"Indeed! You must have ridden as though Stheno herself were chasing you!" Fausta exclaimed from where she stood near the entrance of the atrium. The painted bust of Aphrodite beside her was dull in comparison. She was breathtaking to behold, her olive-toned skin radiant against the deep maroon of her stola. The light from the open air compluvium above glinted off the gems adorning her ears, neck and those in her hair. With outstretched hands, she reached for Crispus.

"Come here, boy. Let me look at you."

He hesitated for an instant, then went to her. Crispus felt his father's gaze heavy on his back as he closed the distance between them. Her practiced smile was frozen in place while his own betrayed his nervousness. He steeled himself with each step. Leaning down, he kissed her once on each cheek. Fausta pressed her face to his mouth as he did it. He could not help noticing how warm and inviting her skin felt under the touch of his lips.

"Hello Mother, how good it is to see you." He took her hand then stepped back in sincere appraisal. "You are as lovely as ever." Crispus dared a glance into her eyes, only to find them staring into his own with quiet amusement. For some reason it angered him, but he dared not show it.

She is a vixen, but I understand why he loves her, he thought. He could not deny Fausta was a beautiful woman. She was sensuous and refined in the way dangerous women so often are – calm on the surface but with fire lurking under her smile. His father was lost in her charms while Crispus could see beyond her seductive mask. He could not fathom why an emperor of Rome would allow a woman to unman him so. Unlike his father, Crispus believed the rumors about her. *She's not half as clever as she thinks*, he told himself.

Fausta continued the farce. "You are too kind Crispus. Mediolanum agrees with us, I think. It is not Rome or home, but it has its amusements I dare say. "

Crispus could imagine what those amusements might be for Fausta. He was about to whisper a sharp reply only she could hear, but his father foiled the attempt.

"I try to keep her entertained – not an easy task," Constantine said. "The first thing she did was demand the palace be razed to the ground and rebuilt!"

Fausta laughed. "You exaggerate, my love. The palace was become a low rent deathtrap when we arrived. It was not fit for the dogs, leave alone an imperial family. I like things more civilized, and my arrangers have done a magnificent job. Just look at it!" She threw out her arms and twirled around. The movement caused her stola to wind against her legs revealing the curves of her body. Constantine was mesmerized. Crispus tried and failed to ignore her.

He cleared his throat. "Yes, um…bravo mother." There was a sardonic lilt to his voice. Fausta arched her brow at it.

His father missed it entirely. "Yes, bravo! My dear, you are marvelous," he said to her. He wrapped an arm around her waist. She simpered, unconvincingly, Crispus thought.

Constantine turned briefly to Atticus. "See to his comfort," he ordered. "The baths have been renovated as well but you should make a trip to the Baths of Hercules instead. It will give you a chance to be among the people. When you return, we shall have a dinner in your honor, in one of the smaller triclinia[15]." He laughed and shot a meaningful glance at Fausta whose cheeks colored a lovely shade of pink at the private joke between them. Crispus rolled his eyes, something that was not lost on Fausta.

She laughed and clapped her hands in feigned delight. "I'll have Messalina organize something special. I am sure Crispus is eager to regale us with the tales of his valor. He'll soon be a rival for you, husband!"

It was Constantine's turn to frown. "Oh, I doubt that – not yet. But he shows promise...great promise." He extended his arm to his wife and together they strolled across the atrium and into an alcove behind it. Heavy curtains hung over the arched doorway. Constantine could not wait. He embraced her on the spot while Fausta pulled the curtains closed with a girlish giggle. Crispus watched them, the bile rising in his throat. Without a word, Atticus handed him a cup of strong wine and discreetly looked away while Crispus drained it.

"Young Dominus, shall I see you to your rooms or will you visit the public baths as your father suggested?" Atticus asked, taking his empty cup. The more Crispus thought about it; the better a relaxing

---

[15] Roman dining room, so called because of its arrangement of three couches around a central table

visit to the public baths sounded if it took him away from this scene. The heart and soul of Roman life were in the bathhouses, and besides, he might glean some knowledge of his father's plans for him while he was there. It did not seem right to ask him on the spot, but Crispus was dying to know.

The Baths of Hercules were only a few years old and built on the same grand scale as the palace. The pale, red brick masonry rose majestically into the sky with rows of marble columns lining each side of the arched entryway. The complex was two stories high with another archway stacked above the lower one to form vaulted peaks on the facade. There were separate entrances for men and women, each facing the street, separated by the archways. A new marble plaque inset above the doorways proclaimed the renovations in honor of Augustus Constantine.

Crispus and the slave boy Rufus entered into the expansive atrium. The same red brick that lined the exterior, framed the inside and the walls were emerald green, covered in sheets of serpentine marble. Attendants waited along them to serve the bathers. The door slave stepped forward to collect the entrance fee. Crispus paid rather than reveal his identity as the emperor's son.

After he had undressed, Crispus tried the caldarium, the heated pool that was always hotter than it should be. As expected, it was practically scalding. Instead of getting in right away, Crispus lay back on one of the stone couches to feel the warm, wet stone against his chaffed skin. He inhaled deeply, filling his lungs with misty air. He relaxed at last. There were only two other men in the caldarium with him, but they soon emerged from the water to move to the laconicum where their sweat-soaked skin could be oiled and scraped clean by bath attendants.

Alone now, Crispus stretched out on the bench for a few minutes and allowed the anxiety of his days on the road to melt away. Later, after a quick plunge into the waters, he walked nude into the tepidarium. Several masseurs stood by with fragrant oils. The two men he saw earlier were already on tables with attendants at work on them. They paid him no attention, but having nothing else to occupy him, Crispus watched them. They were middle-aged, clean-shaven with the neat haircuts favored by the upper classes, but that was where the similarity ended.

The man lying nearest to him was tall, and dark-complexioned with the stiff soldier's bearing Crispus knew anywhere. Across from him, the other man lay with his considerable bulk pouring over the edges of the bench while the slave attending him struggled to knead his doughy back. He looked exactly like a skinned boar, roasted pink and oozing juices. The slaves poked and prodded while the two men continued their conversation. Crispus lay down on his own bench and listened absentmindedly while a slave boy went to work pouring oil over his shoulders.

"I swear to you Silvanus," said the portly stranger. "I will not do it. How can I consent to so rotten a match for my daughter? I cannot abide Cornelius Gallus! I would be doing Pompeia a tremendous disservice to marry her to that murderous man, and I do not need his patronage nearly so much as he needs her dowry!"

Silvanus replied, "Porcius Vibulanus! You offer me insults? Gallus only asked for my help because he admires your daughter and I only give it because I believe him sincere. He was as solid a Roman as you or I during our army days. You will not live forever, my friend. Do you want to leave your daughter unprotected in these uncertain times? Who better to watch over her than a seasoned soldier?"

"So you say, but that man is too brutal! Pompeia is afraid of him and I do not blame her. Over the evening meal, he recounts his gory exploits slaughtering Christians as though it were idle conversation fit for dining with women. Or men for that matter, I don't appreciate hearing about murder over my soup. He is truly odious; I will not sentence my daughter to a miserable life just to improve my own!"

"I cannot dispute the man is unduly proud of his blood games but the blame is not his alone. Maximian rewarded the savagery, if you recall. Gallus does not realize yet that times are different under Constantine, but your daughter need have no fear of him, Porcius. The Vibulanii name still carries weight. He would be insane to abuse her."

"My thoughts exactly, he is mad besides being a homicidal wretch. And I know this much, should Maxentius win this war, and I expect he will, Gallus will be rewarded for his atrocities. Constantine is not the great conqueror you and the rest of the city imagine him to be. He will fall, and the butchery will go on as before."

"That's doubtful on both accounts. Maxentius cannot hope to defeat Constantine on the field, he is badly overmatched. Constantine is as excellent a general as his father, and his son Crispus is being groomed behind him. There is stability with their house in power. Did you not hear that Crispus is coming from the Rhine to attend the Meditrinalia in a few days? There are whispers that Constantine plans to name the boy Proconsul for this coming year. Imagine that, Proconsul! Constantine's house will be in power for generations to come, my friend. Do not gamble on Maxentius to prevail."

Porcius huffed, "Stop now while I still respect you, friend. That boy is barely old enough to shave or know a woman. Tell me you don't approve."

"He has managed to hold the Rhine and distinguish himself in battle many times. Constantine is no fool, I expect he knows what he is doing and the people will agree with him."

"Crispus is interesting, I will grant you. He is even the sort I could consent to marry Pompeia." Porcius said. "He is clearly ambitious, with an excellent name, and what's more he is not a degenerate murderer. No one will blink an eye if Constantine names him I suppose. Though I still say Maxentius will ultimately triumph and Gallus will never change his ways."

Crispus lifted his head at this. The well-fed backside of the man was directly in Crispus' line of sight. Despite the source and the scenery, Crispus' heart leaped in his chest at the compliments. He loved to hear the people speak well of him.

"In any case, you cannot deny that eligible bachelors are scare, regardless of who wins the war. Do you still disagree with Gallus for Pompeia?"

"I'm sorry, but my answer is final. Gallus need not bother approaching me about it."

"Well, that is disappointing, but I have a feeling he will still broach the subject with you. He is quite taken with Pompeia."

"I will tell him myself if he dares ask me; but I'm relieved we understand each other. I would not want to see our friendship tarnished because Gallus cannot have my daughter." Crispus looked over to see Porcius sitting up on his table as he spoke with Silvanius.

"Oh, I understand completely." Silvanus said, sitting up as well. "Tell me something though. What makes you so sure of Maxentius when Constantine is clearly the better general?"

"Constantine cannot tie his sandals without his father. Maxentius has the numbers and they do not lie. When lions fight, size and confidence are the deciders."

"Constantine will surprise you. He has lost his father, yes. But he is bold and intelligent and his son is too. Mark me; the boy will be his savior."

"We shall see. He has plenty of raw potential and it would be a shame for it to go to waste on a losing cause." Porcius said in a bored voice.

"Greatness needs nothing else! Well, I must go. I'm expected at Gallus' house for cena. I will give him your reply." Silvanius hopped down from his table and headed for the clothing room. On the way out, he called back over his shoulder, "Til the Meditrinalia!"

Crispus was glad he was gone, he had heard enough. His heart was pounding, and a happy thrill ran down his spine. He hoped the men were sincere. It crossed his mind they might have been a plant by Fausta to toy with him, but then he dismissed the notion as beyond her wit. Later when he returned to the palace, he felt like a new man inside and out.

There was an unexpected calmness in his spirit. Soon he would have to go back to the war, but for today, he could enjoy his accolades at least. In the vestibule, Crispus paused to look around him. *Everything here will belong to me one day*, he marveled.

He contemplated going to his rooms, but an aroma wafting from the kitchens stopped him. The delicious smells of roasted duck and lamb hung thick in the air, and the sounds of laughter and clattering cups and plates floated along with it. Something in the voices he heard startled him. Not believing his ears, he raced through the atrium to the small room where Constantine and Fausta had disappeared earlier. Crispus laughed aloud at whom he found there.

"Licinius! I did not know you would be here! Let me hug you cousin!" Licinius II was the son of his aunt Constantia and Licinius, the Augustus in the West. He lay on the couch nearest the door, a walking stick at his side. He ignored it when he rose to his feet and walked stiffly toward Crispus while Constantine and Fausta watched from the comfort of their shared couch.

Crispus swept him into a tight embrace. "I only arrived a few hours ago. How did you know I was here?"

"I followed my ears. The rumors have been flying all day. The 'Lion of Gallia has come to Mediolanum'. Everyone in the city is enraptured, but I suppose it's because they don't really know you" he grinned, and winked.

"Or you. If they did, they would know their daughters are not safe around you." Crispus stepped back a few paces. "You look good, cousin. I'm glad to see you're not sulking over your war wounds. Though, I missed your litter bearers at the door. Did you hobble all the way here?"

Licinius pretended to be offended. "A fighting man like me riding about in a litter? Wouldn't do! My vanity would never allow it." He touched the long scar running down his cheek. "I must maintain appearances, no? For the most part, I'm healed. All I really need is a little action to knock away the dust that's starting to gather on me."

"Well, we miss you in Treverorum. The raids have only gotten worse since you have been away. I need you with me. How much longer will you be gone from my side?

"The medici tells me I can return to the legion in another month or so. Sooner if I have my way about it."

"The men have missed your bawdy stories of tavern wenches around the campfires. I can't imagine why..."

Constantine leaned forward and plucked a spiced pear from the mouth of a roasted boar sitting on a platter before him. "Enough! Crispus, Licinius, sit. Take a cup. Later you may exchange your scandalous stories the empress need not hear them now."

Constantine leaned forward again, this time to nuzzle his wife's ear. Fausta laughed merrily, pushing him away while Crispus promptly lost his appetite. As the meal wore on Fausta lead the conversation, doing what she did best. She flirted with Licinius and Crispus both, cajoled her husband and delighted them with her infectious laugh. Licinius joined in after a while and even Crispus began to thaw under her smoldering charm, unconsciously leaning forward as she spoke to him. Finally, a lull in the conversation provided Licinius a chance to deliver news that broke Fausta's spell over them.

Licinius chewed at a morsel of lamb and motioned for more wine. Speaking through a mouthful, he mentioned their old tutor, a client of Constantine who had educated both Crispus and Licinius in Greek philosophy as boys. "Lactantius sends you his best by the way. I had a letter from him last week. We should visit him while you are here." Licinius speared another slab of meat. He shoveled it into his mouth greedily.

Crispus shook his head at his cousin, a professed noble. The time on hiatus from the legion had not improved his manners at all. "Nothing would please me more. He wrote to me several months ago, but I have not had time to reply. A surprise visit would make up for it, I think. Perhaps tomorrow or the day after would be best? Is he still living with his aunt in Laus Pompeia?"

"He is, though neither Laus Pompeia nor Mediolanum suits him. I think he would have returned to Nicomedia by now if your grandmother Helena were not away. He tries to stay close. He feels it's his duty to watch over all of us in her place."

"Grandmother is away?" Crispus said in surprise. No one told him she was traveling. At her age, it was dangerous.

Constantine answered him. "She has

convinced herself she has some divine mandate to find the true cross of Christendom. It was an ill-advised adventure, but even I could not dissuade her. She has been in Judea for some time now."

"Really, my love," Fausta said. "I don't know why you didn't put a stop to that nonsense from the start. The emperor's mother roaming about the empire, looking for an old piece of wood? It was more than ill advised. She's a plain foo for doing it!"

Crispus and Licinius exchanged shocked expressions. Crispus looked to his father, expecting to see some correction.

"My dove, you should not say that." Constantine ran his hand over her cheek in a caress that should have been a slap, Crispus thought.

Crispus adored his grandmother. Seeing that his father intended to do nothing about the slight against her, he took the matter in hand himself.

"I should think you would use more care in speaking about my grandmother. She is a virtuous woman not deserving of being labeled a fool." He looked pointedly at his father.

Constantine did not respond. Instead, he concentrated on his wine. Fausta looked at Crispus and Licinius, a smug grin on her pretty face, as though she were Aphrodite being awarded the golden apple.

Crispus could stand no more. He rose to his feet. "Excuse me, Father. I'm tired from my long journey. I'll take my leave now, if it pleases you."

Constantine looked up briefly, "As you wish, son. You have earned this repast from blood and battle. Come to me in a few days. There are some important matters we should discuss."

Crispus made a show of leaving them. He offered a bow to his father and stepmother. "As you say, Father. Goodnight to you both."

Licinius rose with him. "I'll come with you," he said. The two of them headed into the east wing of the palace where Crispus' rooms were located and they could have some privacy.

As soon as they were out of earshot of Constantine, Licinius spoke up. "Forgive me. I don't like to meddle, but I'm stunned. Uncle Constantine says nothing when she disrespects his mother? I wonder if there is any pride left in him at all!"

Crispus shook his head. "For the sake of everyone, I hope when he leaves Mediolanum for the battlefront he will come to his senses about that woman."

"Hope yes, but I won't be surprised if the opposite occurs. I've seen it before. Fausta is the kind of woman to make a man forget his reason." Licinius added, in bitter acknowledgement of her skills.

They came to Crispus' rooms. Atticus had made certain a healthy supply of Sestian wine wait for him. "Sit down and drink with me. Here at least we don't have to watch him fawning over her." Crispus said removing his cloak. He and Licinius settled into comfortable seats that allowed them to spread their legs out in the otherwise cramped room.

Crispus and Licinius talked long into the night. They laughed, drank their fill and relived their most daring battles and boyhood adventures. In particular, they could now find humor in the battle that landed Licinius in Mediolanum, far from the warfront and the action he craved.

Licinius gave his wounded leg a lighthearted

pat. "–And for this I'm condemned to be my mother's pet again. I bought her a dog to love in my place, but she decided I was better company."

The injuries he spoke of that forced Licinius to his mother's villa happened in Turin the previous year. Constantine's army had won the day but Licinius was trampled and speared by Maxentius' retreating forces. If not for Crispus attacking from behind and dragging him away, he would have been dead on the spot. Licinius was determined to repay the debt one day.

"She's wrong – about the animal at least, you should have bought her a pet weasel instead, the resemblance would have been enough to sway her!" With wine and food in his belly, Crispus found everything Licinius said to be high comedy. He grinned, truly happy to be home.

The next morning they rose at dawn to make the trek to their old tutor. It was perfect weather for a ride through the countryside. The landscape changed from grassy plains plucked of their harvest, to hills and vast forests, as they moved further south. They arrived in the sleepy little village of Lau Pompeia after a few hours and went directly to the opulent villa where Lactantius had been a guest for the better part of a year.

The villa rustica[16] was easily the largest residence in the town and sat on a small hill. It was enclosed behind an iron gate to keep out the local peasants. The villa and accompanying fields bustled with movements as slaves paused their work to watch with curiosity as Crispus and his cousin made their

---

[16] Main house of an Italian estate or plantation

way up the circular path towards the main house.

When the men were shown inside, Anthimus, Lactantius' beloved body slave greeted them warmly. Anthimus was only a few years older than the cousins. He had grown close to them while they lived in Nicomedia. Anthimus escorted them into the peristyle to await Lactantius with a happy bounce in his step. Only minutes passed before Lactantius came to them, wispy, gray hair flying about his head and his tunic nearly tripping him as he toddled into the garden. The expression on his wizened face morphed from confusion to happy surprise.

"Anthimus, you hound! Why didn't you tell me my boys have come to visit me? What joy! I have been longing for stimulating conversation. We shall see what you recall of your lessons!" Anthimus poured him a cup of wine adding a generous amount of water to it as Lactantius settled himself onto a padded bench.

Licinius grinned. "I've brought you a captive audience." He waved an arm in Crispus' direction. "I had to promise him you would not try to convert him to that cult you follow to get him here. So no lectures!"

Crispus laughed. "Licinius, you lie! Don't believe a word of it, Lactantius. I was happy to come!"

"Oh, I am well acquainted with Licinius' sense of humor. Truly, I am overjoyed to see you both alive and well." He stopped to give Licinius a full once-over before he added, "–For the most part – but apparently you're greatly improved, Licinius! I have never ceased praying for you both!" He looked pointedly at Licinius, "–And you may call my faith a cult, but you're benefiting from my prayers!"

Licinius refused the bait. "As you say, Lactantius. I know better than to dispute you. My knuckles still tingle from being hit so many times over the years."

The three of them enjoyed the sunlit garden together in a familiar intimacy. They debated politics, the empire at war, and when all other subjects were exhausted, they turned to religion. Lactantius had been a Christian for many years and he shared his beliefs with the family. Helena was the only member to convert, but the others accepted Lactantius' faith as a presence in their lives, as much a part of him as his wiry frame and protective nature.

"I've had a letter from your grandmother, Crispus," Lactantius said. "She expects to locate the holy relics very soon. I receive letters from her every month about her progress."

"I'm glad someone is in contact with her. I've been so preoccupied with the frontier that I never have time to write letters. I had no idea she had gone to Judea until my father told me yesterday."

"It hardly seemed possible or well-advised, but she was determined. I have been praying and fasting since she left. When I leave Laus Pompeia, I should like to join her, but my students may take exception. I have been gone from them too long as it is."

"When are you leaving?" Licinius queried.

"In a couple weeks I think. There doesn't seem to be much need for me to remain. The emperor will be leaving within a few months and you're obviously progressing well."

"That I am. Even if I doubt their effect, I

appreciate your prayers," Licinius said. It was as much of a concession as Lactantius, or anyone else for that matter, could expect from him.

The afternoon faded away and still they debated on. Crispus and Licinius were no match for their learned teacher, but they did enjoy trying to outwit him at every turn. The following morning Crispus and Licinius left Laus Pompeia and headed back to Mediolanum. Picking up where he left off, he rained colorful images of his exploits in Treverorum into Licinius' news-thirsty ears.

Crispus and Licinius reached the city in the afternoon. They rode to the palace together without fanfare this time and parted ways at the iron gates. Forever soldiers, they blessed each other with an oath learned from their fathers.

Licinius began it. "Goodbye cousin, till I see you again. For blood and empire."

"From now until death," Crispus finished with him.

As Crispus turned to walk away, a strange feeling of melancholy came over him. He had recited the oath many times since he first spoke it as a boy. This time was different. There was a finality that was not present before. A new and dangerous threat was coming that Crispus could only identify as a disturbance in his spirit. An oppressive feeling nagged at him like an ill-fitting breastplate across his chest.

Just nerves, he chided himself, dismissing it aloud. "Be calm. There's no mischief here. You're imagining things that do not exist."

Chapter Seven

Sons & Lovers

Two nights before the feast, Crispus was in his chambers when soft knocking sounded at the door. He was alone, having sent away the serving girl he allowed to seduce him for a second night in a row. The hour was late. The entire palace was asleep except for guards patrolling the grounds. Crispus sat at his desk, reading Homer play by candlelight. He rose from his chair in annoyance. Who in Hades could be looking for him at this hour? He straightened his tunic and wrapping a cloak around him, he opened the door. No one was there and the corridor so quiet, empty and dark that he thought he imagined the knocking.

Crispus stepped into the inky black of the corridor. The only light came from a small opening in the ceiling that poured down moonlight in streaming waves. A figure materialized from the darkness and slipped past him into the room so quickly that Crispus could see only red hair and a long neck, glowing alabaster pale in the dim lamplight. The figure turned, Fausta's pet slave stood before him.

Crispus found his voice. "Messalina! What are you doing here?"

"Young Dominus, please," She whispered. "My lady needs to see you right away!"

Crispus hesitated. "What is so urgent the empress comes for me so late? Where is Father? If this is about his proclamation, it is not formal yet! Fausta has lost her –

"–That is not why she calls you to her and I cannot say more. Will you come?"

Something about the conspiratorial look in her eyes intrigued him. He paused. What could it hurt to humor her? "Very well, take me to her." He grabbed a lamp from his desk and a cloak against the cold.

Messalina led him out into the corridor. The lamp did little to penetrate the gloom. As they crept along the empty walkways, Crispus tried to stifle his amusement. It occurred to him Fausta knew what his father's plans would mean for her. Coming on the heels of his victories, she and her children would soon find themselves ranked behind him.

She wants to make peace with me now, but I won't make it easy for her. I'm not my father; he thought as he followed Messalina to the upper story of the palace where Fausta kept her rooms.

Messalina moved silently, stopping several times along the way to pull him into the shadows as they encountered Praetorian guards. She led him across a small outside portico to a circular stairway cut into the marble. They climbed the spirals of the stairwell to arrive at a large door framed in light. The door led to another short walkway. Golden lamplight flickered off the walls and illuminated the richly detailed frescos along the way.

Each set depicted a different story from

Rome's legendary past, Hercules and Cacus locked in mortal combat; the rape of the Sabine women, Tarpeia betraying Rome and several others. Finally, Messalina stopped in front of a door midway down the corridor. She entered quickly, pulling Crispus with her. As soon as he was inside, she fled the way they came, leaving him alone in the room.

The first thing he noticed was the stifling heat. The source was an oversized labrum[17] that sat steaming in a corner. The air was an intoxicating mélange of vanilla and myrrh. He was in Fausta's private cubiculum[18], a place he imagined in forbidden moments but had never seen. In front of him was her bed, an exotic affair of ivory and gold inlaid over an oak frame carved with lilies and roses, her favorite flowers. The bed was covered in furs and silks with soft cushions spread across it. Issa lay underneath the bed on her rug, growling and baring her sharp little teeth at all comers. Crispus ignored the troublesome beast but his foot itched to give her the kick she earned long ago.

A smoldering brazier near the open terrace provided the only light in the room. Fausta stood just outside of it in shadows, taking in the night sky. She came into full view as he stepped closer. Crispus paused, taken aback by beauty he liked to pretend did not exist but could not deny.

Fausta wore a thin palla[19] draped across her shoulders and a gossamer knee-length shift tied onto her by woven strings. Her hair was loose and flowed

---

[17] A water-filled basin common in Roman baths
[18] Roman bedroom
[19] Robe worn by women like a cloak or shawl over their dresses

over her shoulders and breasts in brown waves. Noting his startled expression, she made a show of clutching at the filmy palla, pulling it tighter around her.

"You sent for me, Mother." Crispus said in a voice he hoped was casual enough to not betray his excitement and nervousness.

She moved closer to him. "Excuse me. I was far away from here. Forgive the late hour, but I had to speak with you."

"No matter, sleep flees from me tonight, I was reading when your girl came for me." Crispus said. He stepped back to keep some distance between them. "What is it you need from me?"

"Why do you look at me so?"

He blinked at her in disbelief at the question. "I think you know why. You bewitched my father and I don't trust you."

Fausta smiled sweetly. "You wound me, Crispus. Can you not understand that I love your father and I'm worried about him? Why would I bring you here otherwise?" Her eyes widened slightly, asking him to believe her. Her expression was almost childlike. Her lips parted and each breath she took was shallower than the last. Emotion was raw on her face. She hovered somewhere between passion and pain, and it was beautiful to behold. In a flash of insight, he thought he understood what drove her.

She's afraid, he thought. He felt compassion for her. She looked away from him, stood quietly until Crispus visibly relaxed, and then started over with more patience.

"Forgive me, Mother. This secrecy is frustrating. Messalina said nothing, so if you please, why am I here?" He tugged at the neck of his tunic. He was nervous and sweating so much it had begun to stick to him. He went for a quip to buy himself some time to sort out what was happening. "So this is why you wear so little? This room is worse than a caldarium."

Fausta indulged him a small smile. "I often overheat my rooms. It keeps my skin soft to the touch and sweet to the taste." Fausta gestured to a set of couches and settled into one of them. She motioned for Crispus to take the other. He did not move, at first. Then taking care, he slowly removed his cloak, straightened his tunic and sat down across from her. He adopted as casual a manner as he could and waited for her to speak.

"I apologize for the intrigue. I had to be careful," she said when Crispus was near the end of his patience. "No one must know I have spoken to you."

The corner of her mouth turned up a bit with a mischievous smile. The effect was charming enough that it softened the hard edge in his voice.

"I still don't know why I'm here."

Fausta gave a deep sigh. Crispus watched as her breasts rose and fell, downy half-moons that whispered of deeper, lower delights and which distracted him from the serious, shocking nature of their meeting. "Your father is very ill Crispus, and growing worse every day. I'm afraid for him."

Of all the things he expected her to say, this wasn't one of them. He was caught off guard. His eyes widened and he sputtered, "What kind of nonsense is that? He has never been in better health! You don't know what you're talking about." He sat back in his chair as caution crept back into his mind. If Fausta noticed the change, she said nothing. Instead, she dropped her hands to her lap before turning them into little fists.

"What's this?" Crispus laughed rudely. "Do you intend to beat me if I don't agree with you?" His anxiety was a palpable thing; he was barely keeping ahead of her.

Fausta slid her chair closer to him. She grasped his hands in hers. "Listen to me! It's not his body, but his mind that draws my concern. He is sullen and brooding much of the time. Never with his men, but with me. It's unbearable to see him so. He has never been this way – has never allowed me to see his pain before now. It worries me. Is it not the same for you?"

"Well, I…"

"Perhaps he sees you as just another soldier…Still, I don't know how much longer he can endure or how long I can endure being caught in the middle watching him. It's all too cruel!"

Crispus could not avoid her gaze. Her eyes on him made him feel out of control; he struggled to focus. "This war has taken its toll on all of us – you more than others, but you're wrong Fausta. We have a divine calling to greatness, to lead. His mind will not break as easily as you believe it will."

Fausta went on. "There is more to it than that I'm afraid. He cries out in his sleep as though all the hounds of hell were after him. He jumps at shadows when he wakes. Please, will you help me?"

Crispus stared, dubious of her claims. "Help you do what…and why should I?" he said finally.

"Because it must be you who goes to him.

Find what troubles him. He holds you high above all his soldiers. He will listen to your honest counsel –"

Crispus stopped her here. "Honest counsel? Counsel him to what? Stop having bad dreams? We are at war."

"Yes, and if he loses his mind to specters and fears, as my father did I won't be alone in suffering for it. It's meant to be a secret, but your father intends to make you Praetorian Prefect and then the Proconsul of the province. If his men doubt his sanity it will mean nothing. You have plenty of reasons for making sure your father is well."

Crispus nearly chuckled aloud. He knew he was right about her and the knowledge gave him confidence. "Sorry to disappoint, but I know all about his plans. I welcome them and so will his legions. If this is your worry, that he will somehow overlook–"

Fausta looked surprised. "You know? Well... that's very clever of you. But listen to me. It is within your power to end this war, Crispus. Don't you see that? Help your father regain his bearings. End this senseless war and his worries. Help me convince Constantine to make peace with my brother." Her wrap fell away just then, revealing her bare shoulders. She pulled it close again. Crispus could not keep his eyes from trailing down her body; but he forced them back to her face.

The woman was speaking nonsense and he told her as much. "I'm a soldier. Father is too. Why would we do anything other than crush our enemies, especially when victory is finally within sight? The idea is ridiculous. I cannot help you."

"Crispus, please! For my children. This war will drag on for many more years without your intervention. You can end it now and save countless lives."

"I don't know what to say to you. I don't agree. I don't know what I expected in coming here, but this is not it," Crispus said with a conviction he did not feel. He rose from his seat. "I don't want to embarrass either of us further. I misunderstood your purpose and I don't want to hear of this again!" He turned to make his escape and forget she ever called him to her rooms.

"Wait."

It just a single word but it stopped him short. Her voice was sensual and ripe with promise. He wondered what she would do, but the answer came soon enough. Her wrap fell open again and this time she made no move to close it. The flickering lamplight in the room reflected off her gold and carnelian earrings, casting red shadows that danced across her shoulders down to her breasts.

While he watched, she untied the ribbons holding her shift together at each shoulder. The pieces fell apart, a treasure box opening to reveal the hidden bounty of Empress Fausta naked to her waist. Crispus traced the curves of her body with his eyes. Her breasts looked heavy, and were curved to fit just so in a man's hands – his hands. He longed to touch them to find out. Her erect nipples were tawny-colored buttons he longed to take in his mouth.

Crispus swallowed hard making a vain attempt to pull his eyes away, but it was beyond him. He fought his exhilaration though, his gaze traveled lower still. Her belly was stone flat with a thin, nearly invisible line of golden brown hair that trailed from her navel, an arrow seeking its target. With one bold manipulation, she had him. He was ensnared better than a hare in a hunting trap.

Crispus could hardly breathe. Everything else in the room went dark, except Fausta sitting within a circle of light, her body an open invitation. Her beauty matched the vibrancy of the fire in the brazier and burned him from within, despite his trepidation. When she spoke, he already knew what she would ask, what he did not know was how he would answer.

"Your father will listen to you. What must I do to gain your support? You and I have been playing this game for too long. I know what you want. You may have it." She stood before him, unashamed of her nakedness. Her body in all its glory was exquisite and though she was doing everything she could to appear vulnerable, he could not miss the defiance begging for submission in her green eyes. That defiance snatched him back to reality; but served to inflame him further. Fausta needed to be put in her proper place.

"Whore" he said quietly through a mist of self-righteous indignation. "My father trusts you! What makes you think I will be a part of this or want anything you offer me?"

Fausta stared with unflinching calmness, then smiled. "Don't you? Because if not..." She made a show of retying one side of her fallen shift, but the other side was still at her waist leaving her breasts partially exposed. She was so close to him now that he could see the pores of her skin, smell her honey-fresh breath, warm and inviting on his face. "Forgive me. You may go...or you can stay here with me. It's your decision what happens now."

She trailed her hand lightly across the tops of

her breasts and her neck. Crispus had a momentary wish that it were his hands making the circuit to her throat but he couldn't bring himself to do it despite that she was here before him and more than deserving of it.

Watching her, he thought of the many times he had wanted to squeeze that narrow column between his fingers and watch the light fade from her eyes. Rather than repel him, the thought excited him. He had trouble looking at her. He felt too dangerous and too reckless. He was not alone. Fausta was as flustered as he by the looks of her. Her lips were full and moist, and her eyes locked steadily on his. They dared him to fear her, to run away from her.

Common sense told him to do just that. Fausta was his father's problem not his, not really, but he could not have moved if saving his life called for it. His feet were rooted to the floor. His mouth was gritty and his chest trembled just enough to remind him he was alive. He swallowed hard but it did not help to clear his nervousness.

Her eyes bright with the beginnings of victory, Fausta went on. "You cannot deny there is something between us. It means nothing if we indulge it this one time and no more. I love your father, just as you do. There is no harm if we promise silence."

"Love him? You speak of love at the same time you seek to betray him? You have a stone heart, woman. I want no part of this." But it sounded like a lie, even to his ears.

"You don't? You pretend to be indifferent, but I see your ambition. I admire it. What you want is yours for the taking, a peace offering between us."

"I don't like evil women. Give me one reason

I should not go to my father right now and tell him what you've tried to do here tonight."

"You could do that – but you won't. We both benefit. I win your support…and you win me."

Crispus tried again to find his strength. "Are you a common prostitute that you have come at me this way? I'm not a customer negotiating with you!"

"–And I am no prostitute. I'm just a desperate woman who loves her family! You are a man who imagines he can tame me. I will allow you to try, that's all."

Crispus looked at her for a long time. Fausta never wavered. She gazed steadily into his eyes. *What nerve*, he thought, admiringly. *But I'll play along. She thinks I'm a silly boy, but as soon as I leave here, I'm going straight to my father.*

He allowed her to grasp his hand and lead him to the bed. She pushed him against the pillows and then lowered her body slowly over his. She kissed him deeply, her hands beginning to explore his most intimate places. Against his better judgment, he relaxed, briefly closing his eyes at her touch. He did not protest when he felt her hands tugging at his tunic, though he knew he wore nothing underneath it. He helped her lift it over his head in a single fluid motion.

He laid back again, naked save for the gold bands around his arms and his sandals. Closing his eyes, he tried to forget how comical he must look right then. He dared not open his eyes again. He did not want to think about what she was doing. It was enough to feel it. Her tongue trailed down the center of his chest. She paused at his navel, tickling it with her lips before moving even lower. Crispus stopped breathing. He felt separated from reality but his ability to protest his break from the real diminished with each flick of her tongue against his skin.

When Fausta finally took her prize in her mouth, when she claimed him despite his false protest, he gasped as the unexpected inferno of wet heat overtook him. Fausta wound her tongue expertly around him. Slowly at first then increasing in speed until a moan he could not prevent escaped his lips. When he was close to the edge of his sanity, she suddenly stopped.

Crispus opened his eyes to find her waiting, staring down at him. While he lay a captive rabbit, she slid down his body. Her inner thigh rubbed against his hips as she sank slowly onto him. The sensation of slipping inside her was like experiencing his first time all over again and nothing else in the world mattered. The consequences of his actions were lost under Fausta's expert hands, she had complete control of him. The battle was lost before it began, and he enjoyed every second of his defeat.

Afterward, they lay beside each other. Crispus was completely spent. He managed to put his clothes back on, to begin the game of pretending nothing happened. But he was not ready to take his leave just yet. His lay back against the pillows with his eyes closed. His mind churned with the full weight of what he had done. It was impossible that he should be here with his father's wife, yet he had allowed it to happen. He understood now why his father could not resist this woman, but he refused to join in his slavery. *It will never happen again*, he vowed.

His senses had only begun to return to him when a white-hot spear of pain seared across his face.

His eyes sprang open. To his horror, Fausta was leaning over him with a small but serious looking blade, poised to strike. She had already sliced him across the cheek once and was about to do it again. He flung her away and tried to rise from the bed, but the cushions and coverlets prevented him. She took another swipe at him; this time she sliced his tunic deep enough to open a jagged cut near his neck. She threw herself on him to press her attack. Crispus was able to grab the blade from her hands, but ripped her clothes in the process.

"What are you doing, you insane woman!"

"How dare you take such liberties with me? I am your empress!" She shouted at him, her face contorted with unexpected rage.

Crispus was both confused and angry as well, "You seduced me, not the other way around!"

He had no more words, not that any were needed. Fausta was dangerously unbalanced, but she had outwitted him. He had been a fool and his only thought was to escape if he could. He worked frantically to extract himself from her bed.

Crispus tossed the blade across the room where it clattered loudly against the wall. It brought Issa from underneath the bed. The pup looked around wild-eyed, but before she could react to the scene, Crispus delivered a sharp kick to her rear. The cur yelped in surprise and pain. She raced back under the bed faster than she came out.

Crispus looked at Fausta, who was still on the bed, ripping at her hair and her already tattered gown. Her mouth was open to scream but she had not yet filled her lungs enough to produce a cry. Her deranged image unnerved him. He made a dash for the door without looking back. In his haste, he left the knife where it lay in the corner. Behind him, Fausta's scream rang out at last. He prayed no Praetorians heard her. He turned in time to see Messalina rushing to the room from down the hallway but kept moving.

With some difficulty, Crispus managed to get back to his chambers. His mind was racing, and he couldn't make sense of anything. Thankfully, he knew where to go for help. Lactantius would have the answer; he was sure of it.

Stopping in his rooms only long enough to discard his ripped tunic for another, he crept as quickly and silently as he could to the stables. Viatoro seemed to know something was wrong. He was calm and pliant as Crispus hastily saddled him. Within minutes of fleeing his stepmother's bed, he was speeding through the dark countryside, heading to the one person he could trust.

Moments later Messalina stood in Fausta's room, giving her report. "He's left the palace, Domina. Just as you thought, I found him in the stables and watched him ride off. And I found this is his rooms." In her hands, she held the ripped tunic Crispus had too hastily tossed aside.

Fausta took it from her with glee. "Excellent! He's playing his part to perfection. How do I look?" Fausta was sitting on the edge of her bed, summoning quick tears. She raked her fingers through her hair, clawing more of it down.

"Exactly as you should, a woman scared and attacked. Your husband will be furious when he sees you." Messalina picked up a small bronze hand mirror so Fausta could see herself.

The face reflected back at her was red and swollen, salty tear trails ran down her cheeks. Her eyes though, surprised even her. They held no remorse in them, no hesitation, so vastly different from the young girl who dreamed of running away. She looked down at her shift torn across the bodice and ripped it at the bottom as well, leaving a jagged tear that ran up her thigh.

"There now, everything is set. Fetch my husband."

Chapter Eight

Running Scared

It was midnight on the Via Aemilia. The ancient roadway running southeast away from Mediolanum was deserted as Crispus raced across its cracked stones. Viatoro's heavy breathing and his hooves against the stone were the only sound for miles in every direction. Crispus' heart beat painfully against his ribcage. The pounding of it in his ears made it difficult for him to think. With each passing moment, he slipped further into a netherworld of shadows and fear where he was a mere spectator, powerless to do anything except run in the opposite direction.

He could not fathom how he had gotten into Fausta's bed nor why he did not get out of it sooner. He asked the question over and over with no resolution. Guilt and shame was a double-edged sword that stabbed him without mercy. He was mortified at having been so easily outmaneuvered, and by a woman. Fine Roman he was and a coward to boot.

He stopped there. *I am no coward. My blood is stronger than that*, he told himself but the words felt hollow as he fled into the night like one. He tried to convince himself to turn around and head straight to his father to tell him what really happened, but it was likely the guards would kill him on sight. Or, could it be possible that his father would hear his side before he decided his fate? Crispus had never crossed his father before, perhaps Constantine would show him mercy.

He pulled up sharply on Viatoro's reins to turn around, then reconsidered and loosened them again. In his confused state of mind, he did that several times before he finally sighted Laus Pompeia. It was a relief to see the village in the distance. At least he could resolve one dilemma; he would not go back to his father now.

The estate where he visited Lactantius just days ago was very different at night. Behind the gates, the sprawling main house sloped down the grassy hill and disappeared into the darkness. There were no guards in sight. Crispus seized the opportunity presented. He tied Viatoro to a tree near the gates, then slipped around to the rear of the villa. He was deciding how to get inside when he saw a door slide open, a few feet in front of him. Quickly, he darted into the darken area beside it. A young woman exited with what must have been a full chamber pot if the smell was any indication. She headed toward a nearby cesspool.

Crispus emerged from the shadows into the dim light spilling from the doorway. The woman heard his footfalls on the gravel walkway before she saw him. Startled, she whirled around at the sound. The sticky contents splashed out and coated the bottom of her tunic. She hardly noticed as her eyes went wide. The woman dropped the bucket and backed away, a scream forming on her lips. Crispus pushed her against the wall, his hand over her mouth.

"I'm not going to hurt you. I need your help. Don't scream, please." he whispered. When she nodded, he released her.

He spread his hands out as unthreatening as possible. "Can you take me to Lactantius? It's urgent that I speak with him."

"Who are you? What are you doing here?" she demanded, her fright drained as anger took its place. She looked down at her ruined tunic, then back at Crispus in disgust.

"Look what you did! Merda[20] everywhere! Get away from here, or I'll call the guards. My mistress doesn't suffer beggars at her door."

"I am no beggar! I am an old friend of Lactantius, and I was a guest in this house days ago. No need for you to disturb your mistress. I am not seeking her. I have come all the way from Mediolanum this last hour to see Lactantius. Tell him Flavius Crispus is here and needs his help."

The woman still looked unconvinced and wrinkled her nose at the putrid scent wafting from the splatters of household sludge clinging to her clothes. While Crispus watched her in anxious silence, she snatched up the spilled bucket and flung its contents into the cesspool. Turning back to him, she weighed her decision. Another eternity passed in the balance. In the end, she motioned for him to stay where he was. Holding her stained garments away from her, she disappeared into the villa.

Crispus did not know whether to run or to stay. All he could do was stand there in the darkness

---

[20] Vulgar term for feces

and hope she would not summon the guards to take him. When she finally reappeared some time later, she was changed into a clean garment and mercifully, she was alone.

"I will take you to him, but you must not make a sound now, or when you leave," she told him.

Crispus breathed again. "Thank you." He whispered, taking her hand. He laid the lightest of kisses to the inside of her wrist. Embarrassed, she pulled away, but permitted him to follow her inside the villa. The woman led him down several long passages until they arrived at a room in the rear of the villa. Before Crispus could knock on it, the door sprung open and Lactantius stood before him, worried confusion plain on his face.

"Crispus! My son, what has happened? Come in, quickly before the household stirs. My aunt Cilia is temperamental about her sleep."

Crispus was relieved to see his mentor. He rushed inside the room. Lactantius had been reading a codex by lamplight at his desk. Crispus took one of the two chairs in the room. Sitting in front of the desk, in a rush born from familiarity and his fear, he began telling the old man mostly the truth of what happened between his stepmother and him. Crispus left unsaid that he a more than willing participant up until Fausta sliced his face.

Lactantius looked at him strangely all the same but did not dispute his account. He examined the wound across Crispus' cheek. "This is not deep but it will leave a scar. You say she attacked *you*…and without cause?"

"Well no, not without cause. Harsh words…and deeds passed between us." Crispus sat up straighter, defensive but not yet hostile to his friend.

"The fact remains she tried to seduce me and when I refused, she attacked me." He wondered how far to stretch the truth then decided that he had no choice but take it to the breaking point. There was no benefit to admitting his complicity. "–And I never laid a hand to her. I ran from her as soon as I was able to get free."

"And then?"

"Nothing else, I came here as quickly as I could." Crispus finished. "And now what? Will you help me talk to my father? He will never believe I'm innocent without your help in telling him."

"With or without me it's doubtful he will believe you. I think you can assume Empress Fausta will say it was all your doing, and that she is completely innocent."

"Of course she will. I know that much, but then what is the answer?"

"It's not going to be easy, Crispus. It's your word against hers, but your father cares a great deal for you, I know that. You will simply have to rely on his good sense to know you're telling the truth."

"But what if he doesn't believe me? He clings to her like a drunkard to his wineskin. His intoxication only makes him drink deeper."

"That is not for you to say, Crispus. Your father is no fool, and you can do no better than the truth."

"Is that the best you can do? I should just go back and tell my father his wife is a whore and hope he believes me?" Crispus sat back in his chair, dejected.

Lactantius came to him. He gently touched him on the shoulder. "Trust me now, as you did when you were a boy. All will be well." Crispus looked up into the old man's serene, honest face. If Lactantius truly believed what he said, he was inclined to believe it too.

"With all my heart, I hope you're right."

"I know I am. Let me pray with you, that you receive the answer you seek."

Crispus could not speak. Tears welled in his eyes, and he nodded with a resolve he did not yet truly feel. He did not know if he believed in Lactantius' Christ, but he longed for the peace and quiet certainty that had surrounded his teacher for as long as he had known him. He fell to his knees as Lactantius taught him to do years before. With closed eyes and a bowed head, he was again a motherless child seeking solace from his teacher and a god he could not see, touch or hear. Now, in his despair he hoped to feel Him as Lactantius did.

"You begin, Lactantius, I don't know how."

Lactantius knelt beside him and started to pray. Slowly at first, then building in momentum, the tutor offered an anguished plea on behalf of his pupil. He cried out a tortured voice that captured the desperation Crispus felt at his predicament. When his mentor finished, Crispus opened his eyes with more hope than he felt since his ordeal began. While Lactantius prayed with him, a strange thing happened. The room grew warmer and his place in the world felt somehow smaller. Crispus felt a stirring in his chest that was missing before, and with it came a feeling that he would survive, that the terror of this night would not stay with him.

"Thank you." He managed to whisper. Suddenly Crispus was exhausted. His body felt the toll of his headlong race to Laus Pompeia, despite his more settled state of mind.

"Take some rest; it is very late. We will leave at first light to return to your father."

Lactantius lead Crispus from his rooms to a small, vacant guest room. Crispus settled himself on a sleeping couch and pulled a light blanket over him. He was so tired, he was asleep before the door closed behind his mentor.

Hours later, he was dreaming of being aboard a large ship, in storm-cast seas, when he was snatched awake by an urgent tugging on his arm. He opened bleary eyes to see Lactantius standing over him, a panicked look on his face. In an instant, Crispus was fully awake. Instinctively he felt at his waist for his gladius.

"What's happened?" he asked in alarm.

"Praetorians were just here. The emperor has ordered your immediate arrest and they're looking for you," Lactantius whispered.

"What! How many? Where are they now?"

"There are at least five of them. Cilia sent them away. She was very upset and put on a grand show of it. They did not persist, but they will be back. I'm sure of it."

"If his Praetorians take me, I won't even be able to see my father, leave alone speak to him. They will throw me into the cellar straightaway."

"Crispus," Lactantius took a deep breath before continuing, "Constantine has ordered you to a summary execution once you are found."

Crispus' face betrayed his shock, then quiet

resignation. "He wants me disposed of quietly I suppose." Crispus shook his head sadly. "I'm to have an extrajudicial execution in a time of war? He's broadcasting our weakness to our enemies. My stepmother has truly beguiled him if he does not even realize how it looks for him to execute a son who has served him so well. No men will remain loyal to him if he kills me, especially without so much as a trial."

Crispus stood to his feet. He began searching around him for the few belongings he had brought with him.

Lactantius' face showed his consternation. "I don't know why your father has done this thing, but you must flee until he comes to his senses. There is no point in going back to Mediolanum now."

"You're right of course. I have no choice. I must run, but the question is where?"

"Think boy. Who would be willing to hide you until we can sort this out?"

Crispus did not need to think long. There was really only one place he could be safe from Constantine. "I can go to my Aunt Zenobia in Nicomedia," he decided.

"Nicomedia?" Lactantius considered the idea quietly for a few moments. "Yes, it should be safe for you there, if you can reach it without being caught first. Wait here. I have something that will help you." Lactantius left the room. He returned a short time later, carrying a roll of parchment sealed with the tutor's insignia in red wax.

"Time is short. Once those soldiers tell the emperor they were refused entry, he will send others who will not be turned away so easily. Take this letter with you and flee to Ariminum. Stay off the main road and get to the house of Felix Cassius, an old friend of mine. He can provide you safe passage to Nicomedia."

"I'll use the lessor traveled trails instead of the Via Aemilia," Crispus agreed. "But who is this friend of yours – how do you know you can trust him with my life?"

"Because I have trusted Felix with my life and the lives of countless others over the years I have known him. He would never betray me – nor anyone I send. His nephew was an early pupil of mine. The family are firm Roman Jews, and been goldsmiths for many years. The nobility know him well. He's discreet and has both the coin and connections to get you to Nicomedia safely."

"But why would he take such risks? How do you know we can trust him still?

Lactantius smiled, "Because he shares my Christian faith and the beliefs I hold closes to my heart. His nephew was one of the first eyes I opened. I hope one day to add yours."

To which Crispus had no reply, at least not one he was ready to share with anyone yet.

Inside the garrison at Mediolanum, two officers argued amid the full-scale search for Crispus. Most nights, the palace grounds were silent at that hour; tonight they sounded with clamor from both Praetorians and every servant, all turned toward the same purpose. The stableboys had been tortured for information, and all of the houseguests, regardless of status, subjected to rigorous interrogations.

The disagreement between the soldiers resulted from an unfortunate report from the search in Laus Pompeia. At issue, who would be the one to explain to their commander the blunder in not capturing Crispus while they knew his location? Neither wanted that perilous chore.

"Why should I have to answer for your mistakes? I wasn't there, was I? My men were properly checking the grounds. It was your men told to search inside the villa, and your men who failed! Do you and your soldiers fear an old woman more than Constantine's wrath?"

The man who spoke was Adherbal, Primus Pilus[21] of Legio Vigesima, garrisoned at Mediolanum. Given his fearsome reputation and intimidating Numidian appearance, he was a favorite of Constantine for military reasons, and of Fausta and Messalina for other more intimate purposes. The man he bickered with was Gaius Avidius. From a high-ranking plebian family, he had a reddish, Gallic coloring, a wild look in his sea-green eyes, and an insolent demeanor to match the arrogance inbred in him, despite his dubious origins. He owed his position to his family ties and he let no one forget it.

Avidius kept to a sternness he reserved for people he did not consider traditional Romans. "You are just as much at fault as I. Perhaps more! You must come with me to deliver this news. The emperor will demand it from you."

Adherbal found his wits and refused his

---

[21] First spear man, a high ranking enlisted position in the Roman army

partner's bluster, "And what should we tell him? That the Nisean stallion was spotted inside the old woman's gates? That your stupid men let an old woman turn them away, all the while my soldiers were busy searching the grounds and couldn't support their efforts? Constantine will put our heads on pikes!"

"Be that as it may, we must tell him...together. If you do not come with me, I will lay the blame for this squarely at your feet in your absence, and you can sort it out later with him."

There was a tense pause but in the end, Adherbal relented. "There's nothing for it. Though, his wrath should land on your head first." he said a small measure of bravado.

Adherbal and Avidius donned their plumed crests and straightened their spines. The two went to the Constantine's chambers where they found the unexpected spectacle of their otherwise stoic leader red-faced and railing at two unfortunates who served as his closest Praetorian guards.

Given that the men Constantine berated were two of his finest, Adherbal whispered to Avidius, "Our chances of getting out of this alive just went lower by half. If your name means anything, now is the time to use it!"

"It won't help you, anyway."

"Can't hurt either. Who know what a man trying to impress his wife will do? I'll take all the help I can get. Look like a soldier here." Adherbal snapped to attention to await Constantine who if anything, increased in rage.

While Constantine heaped abuse on his men, Empress Fausta lay on a lounge, the epitome of a victim. Her servants surrounded her, propped her with pillows. She held her face in her hands, sobbing away in contrived misery.

Messalina stood over her with a tall cup of watered wine. She pressed the cup into her mistress' hand, concern furrowing her brow. Looking up from the wine, Fausta watched while her husband paced the room. She smirked behind the cup while hardly contained rage poured from him.

His men had never seen him so angry. When their turn came, Adherbal took a deep breath then began, "Sir, I have a report for you." He lost his voice for a moment, but quickly recovered. "It seems your son has been located in Laus Pompeia."

"You captured him! Where is he? Bring him to me."

"Ahh, well sir…please, begging your pardon… but master Crispus is still at large. The men dispatched to search the villa where we found his horse, were turned away at the door while others searched the grounds. At some point in the night, he collected his horse and absconded." The room went still and silent; even Fausta's sobs lessened. All eyes were on Adherbal, including those of Avidius, who cowered behind him.

"Explain yourself," Constantine said with deadly calm. Violence hung in the air, an unspoken promise as the centurion struggled to describe the mistakes of the night. Avidius looked skyward in a silent petition as he hoped Constantine would be merciful. Adherbal turned around to him, seeking help from his fellow centurion. Avidius looked away unable to provide any, his pedigree would be useless to either of them, that much was clear.

Plunging ahead, Adherbal kept talking, finding

and discarding words, repeating himself, he stammered through his tale. After several minutes of listening to him, Constantine impatiently held up a hand to stop him mid-sentence.

Constantine moved slowly closer to his soldiers. His iron jaw looked even more so. He came inches of them and spoke with unmistakable menace.

"Find him. If you show your faces here again without my treacherous son in tow, I will punish you in his place. I will have the both of you scourged and crucified. No tale you spin will be sufficient to keep you safe. Do you understand?" With a curt nod of his head, he dismissed them.

Glad to still have their lives at least, they returned his salute and scurried away. Constantine ordered his remaining men out as well. Only three of Fausta's servants remained behind to tend their mistress. Constantine turned to his wife, who was still reveling in her tragedy, and seeking comfort.

"My love, I swear Crispus will pay for what he has done. I will see it done myself!" He touched Fausta's face. His hand nearly covered it, but he was gentle as he ran his rough fingers across her temple and down into the wild mass of her hair. Moving behind her, he wrapped his arms around her and laid his mouth lightly against her slender neck.

"Leave us." He said. The remaining servants including Messalina obeyed instantly, leaving Constantine to comfort Fausta alone. Messalina pulled the door closed behind her, but not before catching her mistress' eye and witnessing her triumphant smirk, unbeknownst to Constantine.

Some hours later Fausta returned from the emperor's chamber to her own rooms. She found Messalina awake, sitting on her bed, freshly remade and waiting for her. Fausta slid in beside her friend and recounted in the colorful language they used only with each other, all that had happened.

"The look on the little bastard's face when I screamed for the guards was worth every risk! He was terror-struck, a rat trapped in the sewer. And you played your part to perfection…he had no idea!" Fausta felt giddy and drunk with the passion of victory. She jumped up from her bed and ran over to her writing table where she dashed off a few lines on a small roll of parchment. After retrieving a few others scrolls hidden beneath her bedding, she handed all of them to Messalina.

"Send this one to my brother," she said, separating one out from among them. "Then burn these. Maxentius needs to know what happened here tonight, but I would not have these messages from him around to provide room for any accusations against me." Messalina secreted the scraps of parchment within a small bag and slipped from the room. She headed to the kitchens, careful to ensure no errant slaves were loitering about before she went into the largest kitchen with her precious scraps of parchment. She tossed the little scrolls into the fire that was always smoldering and left as quickly and silently as she entered.

Despite her precautions, Messalina's actions were not secret. Someone saw her. In her haste to return to the warmth of Fausta's bed, Messalina did not wait to be sure the scrolls burned or that no one had followed in her wake.

Once she was gone from the kitchen, a withered little woman emerged from the shadows where she had been resting before finishing her night duties. After quickly checking to be sure that Messalina was gone, she grabbed a poker to save the scraps before they burned away. As luck would have, the fire was nearly out and the parchments only burned around the edges. She brushed off the few ashes left on them and stole away into the recesses of the palace with the fruits of her determined labors clutched in her hand.

ORDER ONLINE AT AMAZON.COM
OR
SYDNEYKNOX.COM

Excerpt from… A Time of Fear & Flight

Rome — Palatine Hill

"And what have you to tell us, boy?" Emperor Maxentius addressed the nervous young army officer. A patrician with an easy future, Tribune Titus Fabius Titianus stood at attention before him. Maxentius sat at his desk with his arms folded expectantly. General Ruricius Pompeianus and a small gathering of priests and officers were with Maxentius in his private study, his war room. They all waited for the tribune to give his report.

"Our spies say Constantine's son is in Ariminum living with a low-born gold merchant and his family. He has not been in contact with his father or any other member of his family as far as we can tell, sir. We think he may be headed further east on a trading ship."

"And what of Constantine? Has he made any attempt to find the boy himself?" Maxentius tossed his feet up onto the edge of the desk. His red leather boots worn only by the men who ruled Rome were new, the leather still supple as Maxentius absently brushed a bit of dirt from them.

"None that we know of sir," Titus said.

"Constantine knows his lack of an answer to the attack on my sister makes him look weak and he's made it a point to keep Fausta in the dark about the search. She writes that he tells her victory is at hand and nothing else." He dropped his feet abruptly, jumped up from his chair and paced anxiously back and forth across the marble floor. His frustration held in check until then, reached the breaking point.

"This is ridiculous! Completely unacceptable. What can be done? Fausta knows nothing, my so-called informers know nothing, and you slugs know nothing! Why do I bother keeping any of you alive!" He scowled around him, ancient men in heavy robes glared back at him. As one, they turned to Ruricius, who was his praetorian prefect and should handle his outburst. To his credit, Ruricius did not look away. Instead he too glared, daring them to find fault with his friend. Most of the men shied away under his withering gaze.

One however, did not.

He was Servius Caepionis, Flamen Martialis, the high priest of Mars. He was annoyed at the summons, but when Maxentius pressed for a meeting with all the flamines, he had no choice but to comply. Such conclaves were becoming more frequent as the war stretched on. Now that his father Maximian was dead on Constantine's word, Maxentius relied on the flamines' counsel along with his generals. It was often a thankless job, and the flamines plotted and undermined each other almost as much as they railed against Constantine. Servius was one of the few who were more than just a religious politician. He genuinely had some battle experience and knew how to win in the bloody high games of war.

"Maxentius, there are many things we do not know and a few we do, and for those we must act on them. Why risk Crispus reuniting with his father? We know where the boy is hiding. Send someone to kill the boy, and the problem is solved." Servius had served in the military under Maximian for many years.

He was a brilliant strategist and never one to hold his tongue.

Maxentius turned to him, his voice thick with sarcasm. "Just kill him? Excellent notion, just how do you propose I do that without Constantine using it against me later?"

Servius disregarded the emperor's rude grousing. "Don't send imbeciles, use someone who knows what they are doing. I know just the man, a Teuton. He's quick, and he's clean. It will never come back to you."

"Surely you do not mean Charietto?" asked Lucius Scipio, the Flamen Dialis. As the high priest of Jupiter, he was the most senior flamen in attendance. He was a quiet man and only spoke when he had something worth saying.

"The same, do you object?"

Lucius was blunt. "Of course I do, any sane man would. Charietto is a savage, neither clean nor quick. To employ such a dishonest rascal is absurd. He will kill everyone in the household and leave a trail of blood straight back to the emperor. Only a fool would trust him!"

Ruricius bristled at that. He had used the man's services himself in the past. "Lucius, your old dealings with the man is coloring your judgment. The incident you speak of was long ago, and in fairness, you forced Charietto's hand. Notwithstanding that one messy episode with your cousin's murderer, he has been very useful. "

Maxentius quieted them both, saying, "If Ruricius says he is the man for this, then I believe him. Send word to this Charietto. Tell him I want the boy's head by the new moon, and I don't care how, so long as the deed does not come back to me."

"What else?" Maxentius asked Titus, moving on before Lucius could stir up more controversy.

Young Titus continued. "Tribune Firmilianus sends word from Judea. Constantine's mother Helena has disappeared. She was last with Macarius, apparently a well-placed Jew and a man of some renown, even here in Rome. There are rumors of some mysterious find she uncovered in Aelia Capitolina. However, she and her people eluded our spies. An old woman and her servants! She has not been seen in some weeks and may have left for Armenia, to the court of Tiridates."

Servius shook his head in disgust. "What manner of spies are we employing? How can we place trust what they say when they have lost her?"

Titus shrugged and went on with his report. "At any rate, this could be important news. What kind of artifact has she found that would cause so much uproar among her people? It must be something of great power or great value."

"She was known to be visiting locations sacred to the Christians. There were rumors that her people found a miraculum hidden in a cave. But the exact nature of what she found, we do not know. We have suspicions."

"And?" Servius said, irritation beginning to show on his bearded face.

"And, sir? We do not know, as I said…"

"The suspicions, fool. What does Firmilianus think she has?" Servius spat out, losing his battle to be patient with the man.

"He thinks it's a cross, sir."

"We're to be frightened of a cross? Why do

we concern ourselves with a piece of wood?" Ruricius said with a laugh.

"The Christians worship it and this one is said to have a power much older, going back to the origins of the Jews."

For once, Maxentius had been listening carefully, he replied, "These Christians are a strange lot. We know not what hidden powers these artifacts may possess. I would know the truth of this."

He turned to his tribune. "Titus, I want you to oversee this Judean business. Send reliable people this time. I want to know what it is Helena has found in that wasteland and where she is. If she is in Armenia now, lean on our friend Maximinus Daia to keep her there. He controls that land." To Ruricius he said, "And you see to the matter of Constantine's son. Hire this Teton you mentioned."

Both Titus and Ruricius stood to take their leave, but Maxentius stopped them.

"Not yet Ruricius, what news on Verona? It's crucial we hold the city. How many legions did the levies on Aquileia and Patavium bring?"

"They have sent only half a legion each, but it is no matter. The city is easy to defend. It sits in the loop of the Adige River. Its fortifications are intact, and the people are firmly in our camp. We can hold it."

"See that you do, Ruricius. The defeat at Brixia was shameful. The consequences of failing again would see your reputation suffer beyond repair and Rome at the mercy of Constantine." Maxentius told him, as though he did not still suffer the shame of his defeat. The prior year in Brixia, Constantine had slaughtered Ruricius' men and sent his army into full retreat. By the time Ruricius regained order, the battle was over, the day belonged to Constantine and Ruricius was humiliated.

Ruricius stood taller as he spoke. "No, I will not disappoint you or myself again. I swear it!" He locked eyes with his friend and emperor.

Maxentius' firm nod sealed the promise between them. "I have complete faith in General Ruricius. This battle will show Constantine that he does not face cowards here."

Servius brought them back to the reality of their position. "In case the opposite proves true, we need to be able to defend Rome. At all costs, Constantine must not take the city from you," said Servius. "In a civil war, the people side with the victors, not the vanquished. They will hand the city to Constantine along with your head."

"Constantine cannot attack if he cannot reach us" Maxentius said in a rare moment of brilliance. "We'll tear down every bridge and leave an armed cohort at every road into the city. We held out in a siege before; we can do it again. While Constantine sits outside our walls, Maximinus Daia will come from the East and we will trap him in between two armies."

Even the constant naysayer Lucius could not argue. "That just might work," he conceded at last.